Never Knew Love

Sammodah

Never Knew Love

This book is a work of fiction. No part of the contents relate
to any real person or persons, living or dead.

Printed in the United States of America

First Printing, 2015

ISBN 978-0692526736

Sammodah Speaks LLC
Union City, GA 30291

www.sammodahspeaks.com

DEDICATION

This book is dedicated to my nephew Dawuan Potter who was murdered in 2006.

Never Knew Love

ACKNOWLEDGMENTS

My God, my God... Where do I start? God is a great place to start, because without Him I am absolutely nothing. God has blessed me, and for that I will forever be grateful.

To my amazing husband and best friend Jason, you have truly been the absolute most supportive person and my #1 fan. You believe in me more than I believe in myself. I love you past the moon and the stars above.

To my grown man son Dy-Lan, you have been with me since I was a child, and you are the most humble, gracious, intelligent, person I know. Thank you for always believing in me when I didn't have the courage to believe in myself.

To my ultimate diva daughter Taylor B, you really are wise beyond your years. Thank you for always listening to me and allowing yourself to be my sounding board. Oh and thanks for finding the first four chapters of this book that I had stashed away for nine years (and no, you are not getting a percentage).

To my little guy Xavier, thank you for teaching mommy how to be a mommy. I really learned what it felt like to be a mom. Thank you for always being so kind and loving to everyone.

To my little princess Kennedy, they said you wouldn't make it, but you came into the world and took it by storm. You give me so much joy, and I'm so happy God picked me to be your mommy.

To the most amazing parents on the planet, Bobie & Geraldine Hunter. I could never put into words the gratitude I have for you two. You guys have always be there for me no matter what bad choices I made. You all have NEVER let me down. I told you I would make you proud one day, and I know reading this has done just that. Stop crying, Dad.

Much love to all of my brothers and sisters, but I must give special thanks to Marva. Without you, I would have never graduated high school. Kim, without you, my life would not have been filled with so much laughter and joy. Damon, without you, I wouldn't have anyone to call me BABY DIV. Thank you for being so supportive of your nephew with football all those years. You guys rock. That's not to leave out Yvette, Felicia, Robin, Alvin, and Paul. I may not see you often, but I admire and love you all.

To my many nieces and nephews, thank you all for calling me Auntie. To my niece Kisha, I really look at you as my sister. We grew up as sisters, and we will always be sisters. Thanks for always having my back and just being the fierce diva that you are. Sorry for stealing all your stuff when we were kids. To my niece Marva, girl we have done some things lady. You were the little sister I never had. I admire your talent, and I'm so grateful to have you as a little sister/niece. To my niece Kimika, I truly love you, and I pray that you know just how much. You have an amazing heart - never forget that. To my niece Knikki thank you for being the most amazing listener. We had many early morning conversations and they helped me get through another day. To my favorite TJ, you should have been my child for sure. You are a grown ass man, and you act so much like me. I love the father you are and thank you for always making me feel like I was the best auntie on the planet. To my late nephew Potter, you were my little brother, and I dedicate this book to you. I told you I was going to be a writer big head and look who the main character is named after. All that talking you did about the girl, I had no choice. I miss you, and I know you would be proud of me.

To my dear friends Brandi Michele, Daneca, Twanna, and Tiesha, you girls have known me for so many years and you have seen the challenges I faced and loved me through it all. Friends, how many of us have them? Me that's who.

To my G-MOM, you are like a 2nd mother to me. You are an amazing G-MOM to my kids and one of the only people that I can just pour my heart out to without being judged. I met you at age fourteen, and you will always be a part of my life.

To Rhonda Mincey, for taking a chance on me to be a major part of your nonprofit organization. You taught me how to run a business and how a lady with class and grace should be. I admired you then, and I admire you now.

To my homeboy Kevin Young, my original teacher in the writing business, for allowing me to collaborate with you in ghost writing and helping you with interviews and for always being a friend.

To my two amazing mentors, Tiphani Montgomery and Azarel for teaching me the game, I mean the real deal. Thank you for allowing me to be a part of the Best Sellers Project. I promise I won't let you girls down.

To all my in-laws in Middle GA, what up Hudson clan! You guys have truly made me feel like family and taught me the meaning of turn up. I am grateful to be a part of a very supportive extended family.

To my editor Val Pugh-Love. GIRLLLLLL, don't you edit my acknowledgements honey! On a serious note, you have been so helpful throughout this process. I can truly say I gained a business BFF – yes, I made that up.

Last, but not least, to everyone who has supported me in anyway throughout my life, I say thank you. I can write an entire new book about all the people that have been there to help me in some form or fashion.

To everyone who judged me, belittled me, counted me out because I was pregnant at fifteen, in the words of the great late TUPAC AMARU SHAKUR, "I ain't mad at cha."

~ Cheers to you all!

Intro

I am at work in a bathroom stall pondering my life. These two tests I'm about to take will determine my future - a pregnancy test and a rapid response HIV test. How did I get here? If I am pregnant, who is the father? Will the baby be my husband's? He is the only man besides my dad and son that I have ever loved, but he betrayed me, so I had to get him back. I hope it's not for my abusive boyfriend that I have only been with for eight months. In such a short amount of time, he has caused me so much drama. Hell, it may be for my baby's daddy who is a straight sucker for me, but I have never been in love with him. He probably isn't even my son's dad, yet here we are again.

The big question is am I HIV positive? If I am, I won't even know who the fuck gave it to me. If I am not, will I continue down this destructive path and leave my son motherless, my father daughterless, and society whoreless? Two stupid tests are left to decide my fate. It's crazy how a little bit of spit on a stick and piss in a cup will be able to determine my future. I am not prepared to be a mother for a second time at the age of twenty-five, nor am I prepared to have my fifth, yes fifth, abortion. Most of all, I am not ready to die. I should just trash this shit and live life. Fuck it. You only live once. That's what my daddy always said. Maybe that's my problem - living for the moment.

Oh GOD, please help me! I really need help. I promise, if you just let these tests be negative, I swear I will stop inflicting pain on myself. I'm an emotional wreck! Will I finally begin to make the right decisions if the outcome is in my favor? Or, will I end my life knowing I added nothing, I mean *absolutely nothing*, to society? The only thing I was good at was manipulating men with my sexual experiences. Is that what life is all about? I guess that's what the life of a whore is like. That is exactly what I am - a low-life, worthless whore.

Gina was right. DAMN, how could she be right? I have slept with men for money, food, handbags, shoes, you name it. I am definitely the ultimate sex hustler. But, is this something I should be proud of? You can blame it on my childhood or growing up in the "hood" or my low self-esteem blah, all excuses. Shit, I had to do what I had to do. I'm at this bullshit 9 to 5 where I am overworked and underpaid. Hell, ask Gina and she'll say it's a "good" job. What the fuck does that mean anyway - a "good" job? Get the fuck outta here. I'm a slave. I am one check away from being homeless and now this shit. I do not need this shit right now. *God, where are you when I really need you?* Well, here it goes - a swab to the mouth and piss in a cup. Will this be the end for me?

Chapter 1 - Childhood

I was born Brea Renee Simms at Cooper Hospital in a small town called Camden in New Jersey. My father was a loving man, but my mother a complete lunatic. From what I was told, the day I was born my mother made it known that I would never amount to anything. How she knew that by looking at my 9lb 2oz, 20-inch frame is beyond me, but it was clear that she had it out for me from day one. Gina had three children by her dead husband before she met my father. My daddy was a hustler. When I say hustler, I mean he did all that he could do to make it happen - like a real man. He was a Jamaican nigga by way of Harlem, NY, so you know he had the gift of gab. He always got what he wanted. He lived in Harlem in the early 60s but got into so much trouble with drugs and boosting, that he found himself in Camden in about 1968, right before the riots. He met my self-absorbed mother on the corner of Broadway and Kaighn Ave which was thriving back in those days. She was a bombshell. She was high-yellow with a body to die for, but she had the nastiest attitude. She used men to get what she wanted.

My dad was the total opposite of my mom. He was black as tar and not very attractive at all. Hell, he wasn't attractive, but he was always dressed to impress. He pulled up on Gina in his 1966 Caddy with the leather interior. She was waiting for the bus and he offered her a ride. She accepted, which was odd for her, and they have been together since. My dad stepped in and took control of her so-called life. She lived in a small apartment with my three brothers, who were all under the age of eight. My dad moved her and the boys into a four bedroom house in the somewhat nicer section of Parkside. This was great for Gina, because finally she did not have to work. Plus, she had a reliable man, so she did not have to depend on her crazy family to help her.

You see, Gina was uppity. Her mom was half white, so she thought that made her better than anyone else. The truth is, she really wasn't worth shit - especially without my daddy. He was a damn good man and the best provider. He did not have any children, but accepted her three sons as his own. My parents were known around town as the perfect couple. Little did the world know, my mom was a basket-case. She was a complete psycho, and she got even crazier after I was born. By the time I was born, all my brothers were out of the house. My oldest brother, Mark, left for the Air Force after he graduated high school. My second brother, Tim, received a full scholarship to attend one of the most prestigious black colleges, Morehouse College in the ATL. The youngest of my brothers, Ronnie, who was seventeen years old when I was born, was leaving for Hollywood by the time I was crawling. They were all determined to make something out of their lives - more than I can say about Gina.

Camden was becoming an awful place to live, and white flight was imminent during those times. There was really only one section that still had a white influence in the early 80s and that was white boy Fairview - mostly poor white trash if you ask me. Despite the turmoil in my neighborhood, my life was great because my daddy worshipped the ground I walked on. One day after school, I came home to a fully decorated room that my dad had one of his contracting buddies fix up for me. See, my dad was the man around town. He had a small restaurant in Camden's downtown section which was actually doing very well. Two rooms in our house were made into one room just for me. I was his only birth child, and I was a beautiful little girl. I had thick, jet black, curly hair with a nice brown complexion as if I were Cuban or Dominican.

My dad told me that Gina never held me. Before I left the hospital, she told my dad to give me up for adoption because she had no clue on what to do with a "little bitch". Of course my dad brushed her off as he often did. He was not an abusive man, but I know by the way he told me the story, he hated her for that. My dad would take me everywhere he went. I barely remember Gina's presence in my childhood, because she was often on a binge or trying to overdose on sleeping pills. She claims I gave her insomnia. How can giving birth to a beautiful baby girl give you insomnia for the rest of your life? Regardless of how Gina felt about me, my daddy would carry me off to the restaurant and show me off to all his buddies. Gina was a stay at home mom ever since she met my dad. I never wanted to stay at home with her, and I think that made her hate me even more. I would cry for my daddy, and he would eventually come and get me. She hated him for that. You see, she was the apple of his eye before I was born. I did not understand back then the extent of the hatred she had for me, but the older I got, the more I understood.

From birth until about four years old, my life was pretty good from what I could remember. At that age, I could really only remember the good and that good was my daddy. When I was five years old, my daddy wanted to send me to a private school in the suburbs, but this sent Gina into a frenzy. Even though she was uppity, Camden was still her home, and she would not allow any of her children to be schooled by the likes of "white folk." I could not understand this, because Gina always made it known that her mother was half white, as if you could not tell by looking at her. She basically told my father that if city schools were good enough for her boys, then it would be just fine for me. What she really meant was, "if my sons who I love dearly had to go to school here, so does this little bitch that I can barely stand." My dad went along as he always did, but I remember the pain in his eyes. At the time, it didn't matter to me which school I attended, but the fact that I had to leave my dad was my concern. I remember the first day of school vividly.

It was a rather cool day. While Gina got me dressed, my dad went to open the restaurant. The entire time I was preparing for the first day, I was so sad because I knew I would miss my dad. On top of that, Gina would be the one taking me and picking me up. She was pulling my hair and fixing my clothes while telling me that if I did not get my act together, the little hood children would kick my ass. She said that I was a goodie-goodie, and they would smell it on me as soon as I walked in the door. I was so scared of her, especially when my daddy was not around. She did not allow me to play outside. She would say it was because there was nothing for little girls to do outside but get into trouble with little boys. I was a child with no social skills whatsoever.

When it was time to go, I ran into my closet. She was screaming to the top of her lungs.

"Brea Renee Simms, get your ass out here before I kick your ass!"

This gave me more reason to run and hide even further into the closet wishing my daddy came home to save me. Finally, she came into my room after searching all over the house. She sat on my bed which was beautifully decorated with all pink lace and lots of stuffed animals that my daddy bought me. I loved those animals. She was on the bed shaking and talking to herself.

She screamed, "If you don't get out here right now, I'm going to destroy your lovely little room!"

I sat quietly, too scared to come out. I could see her shadow moving through the closet door as she exited my room. I thought the coast was clear, but as usual, I was dead wrong. She came back into my room with a big knife in her hand. By this time, I was looking through the small holes in my closet door to see what she was going to do. While I sat silently crying, she started cutting off the heads of my stuffed animals, one by one.

As she detached each head, she angrily said, "Die bitch die."

I started to cry out loud causing her to open the closet door. When she saw me sitting on my closet floor with my knees pulled to my chest, she grabbed me and put the knife to my throat.

She started shaking me and saying, "I told your stupid black ass to get ready to go, so let's go you little bitch!"

I jumped up and ran to my bed to rescue my prized stuffed animals, but it was too late. She had taken the heads off of every last stuffed animal. It had to be at least fifty of them. This is when I realized that I hated Gina and did not want to be left alone with her. Ever.

After seeing that my stuffed animals were gone forever, I decided that going to school wasn't such a bad idea, because anything was better than staying with her. We did not speak during the entire four block walk to the school. I just wanted the day to be over so I could see my daddy. I guess I thought him up, because my daddy pulled alongside us while we were walking.

"Hey, you guys want a ride?" he said.

I was so happy to see my daddy that I ran to him, screaming his name and jumping up and down. Before we left the house, Gina had told me that I better not tell my dad what happened in my room, so I just got in the car without saying a word of it.

We pulled up to the school, and for some reason I wasn't nervous. I was just ready to be away from this crazy lady that gave birth to me. Gina and my dad walked me to the line, and she had the nerve to kiss me. I was in shock. As my daddy pulled off, a feeling of sadness and loneliness came upon me. *Why would my daddy not know something was wrong with me?* I thought to myself. I felt so empty. Surprisingly, school was okay. All I really remember was playing and eating snacks. I loved to eat snacks. As the day started to wind down, I dreaded going home with Gina. I'd much rather stay at school. She was a disgusting person in my sight, and I did not want to be around her. The school dismissal bell rung, and I walked outside with a lump in my throat and tears in my eyes.

When I looked up, Gina was waiting for me like a thief in the night.

My teacher said, "There is your mom."

I thought to myself, *she's no mom.* She walked over to get me, and actually hugged me and asked about my day. At this point, I was totally confused. This could not be the same woman that only a few hours earlier had taken a portion of my life by destroying my precious stuffed animals. She was really fucking crazy. I knew that at age five. However, she did not act crazy around other people, and everyone thought she was the perfect mom. She grabbed my hand, and we walked the short four blocks home, but it felt like an eternity.

My daddy was there when we got home. I was so happy and relieved to see him. He asked me about my day, and then a look of disappointment came over his face.

He said to me, "Brea, baby, why did you turn your room upside down like that? And, you had a knife. You could have really hurt yourself."

I looked at Gina, praying she would tell the truth.

She looked at my daddy and said, "I told that little bitch to get ready for school, then she attacked me and ripped apart her room."

I cried out, "Daddy, she did it! I swear!"

He told me that I needed to be truthful and that lying is a major sin. I cried my little eyes out, and I couldn't breathe. I could see that he felt bad for me, but I never knew if he believed her or not. It seemed like Gina had a curse on him. She had total control over my father. I lost a lot of respect for my father that day. I thought he was a real man, so why didn't he protect me?

As time went on, things began to take a turn for the worse. My father's business was not doing well at all, so Gina was arguing with him more and more. My father had never been a heavy drinker, but I noticed that he began to drink a lot more and very often. I had to be about eight years old when my oldest brother Mark came home from the military. I really did not know him, since he was gone most of my life. Mark was very handsome. My mother always made it known that she was so proud of all her handsome sons. She always told me that I wasn't pretty because I was too dark. The funny thing is, I am the same complexion as my brother Mark. We actually looked very much alike. Now, I do not know this to be true, but I would swear he was her favorite. She would brag about him as if he were the damn president of the United States. He was the prize in her Cracker Jack box. She would always make it known to me at that early age that I would never be as good as her sons. It didn't even matter to her that I had managed to do very well in school among other things at that point.

About a week before Mark was due to come home was when Gina shot my dad. She had been preparing a huge party at the local community center for my brother. He was well known and very well liked, so everyone was going to come to the party. This party was going to cost my dad a few thousand dollars, but Gina had no concern with that. All she wanted to do was impress people and show off how she could outdo anyone with her parties. I remember my dad telling her that he did not have enough money for her to throw this lavish event. She cursed him out and told him that he "better find it." Her son was coming home, and my dad had better do what he had to do to make sure she had the money she needed. She had the filthiest mouth. As pretty as she was, her fowl mouth could disgust even the manliest of men. My father was so stressed out.

What I did not know at the time was that my dad had filed Chapter 11 bankruptcy, because the business was failing and he had so much debt. Gina knew this, but she did not care. My dad had taken a long ride the day she shot him. When he came home, she was ready for him. I had been upstairs in my room playing. I always tried to stay in my room when I was alone with her. When my dad came home, she was cursing and screaming and telling him that she needed the money for this and that and she needed it immediately. For the first time, my dad was taking up for himself. I could hear him yelling back at her. He told her that he did not have the money, and if he did, she wasn't getting it. By the tone in his voice, I could tell he was very drunk. My mom was enraged at that point and everything went quiet.

I remember her coming upstairs and returning back downstairs. I was smiling and thinking my dad had finally won. I crept to the top of the steps to see what was going on. At that very moment, that bitch shot my dad right in his leg. I saw my little eight years of life with my dad flash before me. I ran downstairs, and she screamed at me.

"Get away from him! What did you do little bitch?" She began to cry out to me, "Brea help me. Help me."

I was totally confused and crying. Even though I hated this lady, she was still my mother and she was obviously in pain. I felt so sorry for her, but I was eight. What was I supposed to do to help her? I walked over to her, and she gave me the gun. She told me to throw it away and call the cops. I did exactly what she said, and when I came back from calling the cops she was by my dad's side. She was crying and hugging him saying she was so sorry and that she loved him. I just stood there in a daze.

By the time Camden's finest had arrived, my dad was not conscious. They came in and took a statement from Gina while the paramedics worked on my father. As they rolled my dad on a stretcher down the sidewalk, I heard Gina telling the cops how crazy I was. She told them that I have always hated her and that I needed help. This twisted bitch had told the cops that I went into my dad's closet, got his gun, and tried to kill her, but my dad stepped in front of the gun and caught the bullet for her. Wouldn't you know they believed her? That day was the end of my childhood. They took me to the station to be questioned, but I never said a word. I never said if I did or did not do it. They let me leave in the custody of Gina, and we immediately went up to the hospital - the same one I had been born in eight years prior.

When we arrived, Gina told me she would do all the talking and that I was not to say a word. It was crazy how demented this beautiful lady was, but if I knew any better, I would keep quiet, and I did.

We were greeted by my auntie, who never really liked my mom but put up with her. She told Gina that my dad was going to be just fine and he wanted to see her. I stayed in the waiting area with my auntie, and she was talking to me and asking me questions, but I knew not to say a word.

When Gina came out, she had a crazy smile on her face - more like a smirk. I asked if I could see my dad, and she nodded for me to go ahead. I was so happy my daddy was alive. When I went in the room, he hugged me, and then opened his mouth only to disappoint me. He said if we told the cops that Gina shot him, she could go to jail. However, if I said I accidently shot him, then I was sure to get off because I was a child. Tears rolled down my face, but I would have done anything to make my daddy happy. Even though he disappointed me, I still loved him more than anything in this world. If only someone could love me like that.

My dad was released just in time for Mark's coming home party, and some party it was. Everyone was there, but I couldn't enjoy them, because I was so sad. Gina had told everyone how I tried to kill her and how crazy I was. She told them not believe me because I was a big liar and I needed to get some help. All of my little cousins at the party said they couldn't play with me because I was crazy and I was going to the nut house. I didn't even know what that meant, but I knew it wasn't good.

I cried in the bathroom for most of the night, and no one came to find me - not even my dad who was wheelchair bond for the next six months. That night, everyone partied and forgot about the lonely little girl inside of me that had just died. That night in the bathroom, I vowed not to be a little girl anymore. I was going to be grown up. No one was going to do me like that again. I would fight back! I would. I hated being lonely. This was just one lonely night in my broken childhood, but I would determine the path I chose from that day forth.

Chapter 2 - Tim Dies

By the time I was twelve years old, shit was crazy. My dad had lost the restaurant, my mom was crazy as ever, all my brothers were home, and I had been to six different psychiatrists who were all trying to "fix" me. My oldest brother Mark had been home since the party. My youngest brother Ronnie came home a year or so following Mark, after his Hollywood career had failed. He came home broke, busted, and gay. My other brother Tim had all the brains, but his money-hungry wife had divorced him and left with their daughter. So, he was forced to come back to the broken city that had been crime infested by 1992.

Our house was jam packed, but Gina was glad that her boys were home even though they were all men by now. Tim was the nicest to me. It seemed like we had a lot in common. I was smart, and I wanted to go to Spelman which was across the street from his alma mater Morehouse. I wanted to be Greek just like Tim, but most of all, we both wanted to leave and never come back. Tim was very bright, and he would write a lot. He lived in the basement, and I would go down there with him for the remainder of the day when I came home from school. I loved my brother Tim because he was somewhat of a loner like me. Mark was a ladies' man. He had like six kids with five different women, and he did not take care of them. Ronnie was a very flamboyant gay man. He was always doing something involving his gay life. I did not care that Ronnie was gay, but his being so open about it pissed me off. Like why did he feel a need to tell the whole world? Tim was a weed head, and he introduced me to smoking when I was twelve. He told me that it would make me feel relaxed when Gina was stressing me out. So, after school I would run home and get blazed with my big brother. Those were some of the best times of my life. I had no worries when I was with Tim, because he was my protector. Gina loved him, but she wished he would not talk to me so much. She knew I smoked with Tim, and she could care less. As long as I was out of her hair, I could do whatever I wanted.

I still never had any friends because I was standoffish, and a lot of girls thought I was corny. I dressed in big clothes, and I was extremely skinny. My gay brother would try to get me to dress up to be a little lady.

He would always say, "You should be kissing boys or something."

I hated all men except for my dad, and now Tim was my best friend. My dad and I never really talked much anymore, because he was at Gina's every beck and call. Ever since he lost the business, he had been working two jobs to keep up with my mother's lifestyle. Her broke ass sons did not have to pay any rent and none of them worked, but my dad had to bust his ass to take care of all of us.

Gina still verbally abused me, but she was popping so many pills and drinking more alcohol than she could stand. Her crazy habits kept me safe from her evil ways. She would sleep most of the day and curse my dad out at night. I was left to do all the housework, because she felt like men should not do chores. My brothers were some triflin' lazy ass negroes. All of them - even Tim.

One day after school, Tim and I were smoking weed like we always did. He must have done some other drugs, because he was talking like a mile a minute. This wasn't like him at all. We never talked much about Gina, because he knew I hated her guts. This day, for some reason, he was telling me how I should respect her and how she was my mother nonetheless. I told him I would never respect her and expressed to him how much hatred I had for her. That day my blood brother, who I grew to love dearly became her. He was Gina. He picked me up by my hair and began chocking me and telling me to never ever talk like that about his mother. I was kicking and punching and biting. I was doing anything to get him off of me.

Even though Gina mentally abused me, she never put her hands on me. What happened next not only shocked me, but scarred me forever. My blood brother pulled my pants down and raped me. He ripped my flower panties with the Tuesday sign off and stuck what I thought at the time was the biggest thing I had ever seen inside of me. I could not even scream. All I could do was cry silently. I was afraid Gina would hear me. She was right upstairs. When he finished, I could not move. I was comatose.

He said, "Sorry, Sis."

Then, he got up and left. I was in a lot of pain. He was not gentle. I was a virgin, and I had never even looked down there let alone let someone put something down there. I began to cry and pray. I knew a little bit about God from the Easter Sundays that we were sent to church.

I knew I had to get up because she would be coming down there soon. I slowly walked up from what seemed like a dungeon to get to my room as soon as possible. I made it to the bathroom and the pain was unbearable. I could not even feel anything from my waist down. I just wanted to die. My insides had been ripped open. I managed to take a shower and get to my room. For the first time in my life, I began to pray and ask God to take me away from my life. Just then, Gina came into my room screaming and telling me to clean up. I told her I did not feel good. For some reason that night, she left me alone after calling me a stinky bitch. I did not care what she called me. I was used it by now. In that moment, I found a small belief in God. Maybe if I prayed more often, He would keep Gina off my back.

The next day was so hard. I left out for school before anyone woke up. I was tempted to go to the nurse and tell someone, but I knew they would not believe me. Everyone knew I was a liar, and Gina made that known. After school, I went to the library and to the park to avoid going home, hoping that everyone would be sleep by the time I got home. When I finally arrived home, it was about 11:00 p.m. It was very late, especially for a girl my age to be on the streets of Camden. I had never come home past 4 p.m. As I walked into the house, Gina tore into me instantly, and of course my dad just stood there lifeless as he always did.

As usual, she called me bitches, sluts, and several whores. I was so annoyed that I began screaming back at her. I had never done that before, but I was tired. While we were screaming, my oldest brother came downstairs screaming at me saying how disrespectful I was. He had some nerve. He paid no bills, but had a new bitch in the house every night. Hell, his ass always cursed at Gina, but she never said a mumbling word to him. I told them all to kiss my ass, even my dad. At this point I was sick of the whole thing. I had been marked as crazy all my life, and I was just raped by my blood brother - my mother's son.

I ran out of the house only to run smack dead into Tim. He turned me around and walked me back into the house. At this point, Gina was screaming to my dad telling him they needed to send me away or she'd kill me, and that I was going to be the death of her. Picture that shit. Her damn son just raped me, and she wanted to send me away. My dad was telling everyone to calm down. Ronnie was not there, he was off being gay as usual.

Tim said, "I will talk to her."

I told him no one needed to talk to me. I made up my mind at that moment that he would not stick anything else in me or he would die. Gina told me if I did not talk to him, she would call the cops and I did not want to go to jail. She was absolutely right. I was a big punk and avoided all confrontation by running. I could run my ass off. Kids would to try to jump me, but they couldn't catch me so they stopped trying. I finally agreed to talk to him, but I would not go into that dungeon again. We went on the front step, and he explained to me how he was so sorry and that it would never happen again. That night, he told me that Gina was not really nice to them either. He also told me how she use to let her dead husband, who was not their dad, molest them while she watched.

Even though Tim had hurt me, I felt so sorry for him. I mean the pain in eyes was intense, and it looked like he had been wanting to get this off his chest for years. I could also see how much he loved Gina. I didn't know that feeling, because I did not give a fuck about her. I was speechless. He had still stolen away the little childhood that I had left, and I was hurting physically, emotionally, and mentally. He begged me not to mention what happened and promised he would never touch me again. He explained how he started some new drug and that is why he had be acting strange. He also told me that he and my other brothers never talked about what happened to them as kids, so I was to never talk about it either. He talked me into staying home that night. I still cared about my brother even though he hurt me. He gave me a greater reason for hating Gina. Why did they let her get away with such brutal treatment, and why did they not hate her like I did? She was the worse mother ever created.

After the talk with Tim, I went back into the house, but no one said anything to me. I went to my room puzzled, yet finally realizing why she was so nice to them. My blood boiled and the hate for her became stronger and stronger. I began to pray and ask God to kill her - just take her away, because she did not deserve to live. We were all messed up because of her. My dad came to talk to me and told me that my mom really did love me. Bullshit. He kept making excuses for her, saying she had issues and that one day I would understand her more. I thought to myself, *SHE has issues? I am twelve years old, and I have more issues than any child my age.* He kissed me and told me it would all be okay real soon. I brushed him off, because he was a sucker and did what she wanted.

The next morning was like any other. I had gotten up to make some breakfast. I managed not to wash up that day. I really did not care about my appearance or my life at all. I actually wished I was dead. Gina came downstairs to make breakfast for the "boys" like she had done often. She called them all to the breakfast table. She was weird like that. She always wanted us to eat as a family. Mark came down first as he always did, then Ronnie with his bright ensemble, but there was no sign of Tim who was usually the first one to be at the table, even before breakfast was done.

Gina yelled, "Brea, go get Tim."

I mumbled, "You go get him."

Then big mouth Mark goes on and on about how disrespectful I was and how someone needed to discipline me because I was spoiled. Picture that. She ignored our arguing and yelled for Tim to come up, but he didn't come. She knew he was there, because she was so nosey and always knew when either one of her "boys" left the house. She went downstairs to get him up. Suddenly we heard her scream so loudly.

"NOOO!"

Mark and Ronnie went running to her. She was screaming like someone had died. I continued to eat my breakfast, because I did not want to be late for school. Knowing Gina's dumb ass, she had probably seen a mouse and needed someone to kill it. My dad had already left, so one of the boys could do it.

Suddenly, Mark screamed, "Brea, Brea get down here fast! Tim is dead!"

I ran to the steps, but I could not manage to go down them.

Ronnie kept screaming, "Brea now is not the time! Stop being a bitch and get down here!"

I could not move. This would become routine in my life, not being able to move or say a word. I ran out the door with my brothers screaming for me to come back. I ran so fast that they could not catch me. I got all the way to the school, and then stopped and decided not to go to school. I played hooky for the first time. I never liked to miss school, because that was the only time I had away from Gina. My mind was racing. I was so scared. I walked around thinking about life and what it would be like to have a normal family.

I finally went home after walking all day, feeling lonely and confused. Everyone was there including my dad. Gina was devastated, but I felt no pity for her. My dad came to me and hugged me, but he didn't say a word. I still didn't know what happened to Tim, and I was too scared to break the silence to ask. I was so sad because he was gone. Why was he gone? We spent the next few days in silence. No one talked about how Tim died, and I sure as hell wasn't going to ask. The funeral was so sad. Gina, of course, was the most distraught. Fake bitch. She was crying and falling all over the coffin. I knew she was sad, but I still believed it was all an act. You see, she was a drama queen, so anything that happened was so devastating to her. She was also drunk and high on pills.

After the funeral, we found out that Tim had overdosed on cocaine. We also found out from his ex-wife that she left him because he had used all of their money to get high, and they lost everything. Naturally, Gina did not believe her or the medical examiner, because her boys were so perfect. She said someone set him up and went into her long list of excuses of why this all was not true. She was fucking delusional. My dad was her backbone, but he was getting older, and the stress of working two jobs and putting up with the abuse he sustained from her was unbearable. He even began to look so old in the face. Gina was wearing him down, but she still looked good with her clothes and jewelry that she could not afford.

For the next the couple of weeks, my house was very somber. No one really spoke, and we definitely did not talk about Tim. I was back at school by now and trying to forget about what had happened to me the prior month, when my life took a turn for the worst. I loved going to school, and I got all A's which was the only thing that I was good at besides track. Gina could not take that away from me. Things at home were so-so. However, for about a week or two, I had begun to notice a very foul odor from my private parts, and I had no idea what it was. I was in the locker room one day changing, and I could smell myself. A couple of girls were going around saying someone stinks, but they did not know it was me. I was so embarrassed, and I knew something was wrong. I was extremely clean because Gina was serious about hygiene. We couldn't even sit on her bed while wearing the clothes we'd worn all day.

I really didn't know much about my body since Gina never talked to me about anything. When I got my period at age ten and a half, she just gave me a pad and told me I knew what to do. I was not stupid, so I knew there was an issue, but what the issue was, I did not know. I had to tell Gina so she could take me to the doctor. On my walk home that day, I was working up the nerve to tell her. She was probably high as hell or sleep, since that's what she did every day after Tim died. I walked through the door with my heart racing. I was so scared as I went upstairs to Gina's room.

"Gina, can I talk to you?"

Surprisingly, she said, "Yes."

I told her I was having "female" issues and I needed to see a doctor. She immediately accused me of being a whore and having sex with the boy up the street. I did not even have time to have sex with any boy. I wasn't even attracted to anybody at this time. Hell, she never even allowed me to go outside, so how she came to this conclusion baffled me. Then again, I wasn't surprised. She went on a rampage about how she did not raise me to be a whore, but she did not even know what was wrong with me yet.

She scheduled me an appointment on that following Saturday for my first pap smear at the local Planned Parenthood clinic. She could not take me to her regular doctor and risk embarrassment. When we arrived at the clinic, it was so cold and crowded. Gina came prepared with her designer sunglasses and her low hat, so no one would notice her. She acted like she was the one with the problem. They called my name, and she insisted on going back with me. They asked me a million questions. I was so embarrassed and ashamed. Finally, they asked me if I'd had sex. Of course I said no, because technically I had not. Plus, I was not ready to expose anything in front of Gina - especially about her dead son.

After I was examined and forced to take a pregnancy test, we went back to the waiting room. The exam really did not hurt, but the fact that Gina was in there with me made it worse. They called us back in - well really me, but Gina had to follow. My heart was in my feet, because I knew something was wrong. When the doctor came in to talk to us, he talked directly to Gina. He didn't even look at me. He told her that I had gonorrhea, but worse than that, I was pregnant. She passed out - as she often did to get attention. She was such a drama queen! I had nothing to say. I had a disease that I could barely pronounce, and I was pregnant by my dead blood brother. This was some shit out of a movie. I did not even cry. I just sat there emotionless.

She cried out, "Brea, why would you do this to me."

I thought to myself, *this bitch is really crazy.*

She was more concerned about her reputation than she was about her only daughter. One thing I knew for sure, was that I was NOT going to have a baby. I never wanted to be a mom, and I definitely was not going to do it at my age. So, when she said I was getting an abortion, I was just fine with that. She never asked me who the father was, what I wanted to do, or even when I'd first had sex. All she wanted me to do was get rid of this baby and do it fast, so I wouldn't embarrass her, like I was the only teen mom in America.

She got me an appointment scheduled four days later to get my first abortion of many more to come. We arrived very early in the morning, and Gina pushed me quickly past all the people holding bibles. I remember a couple whispering about how young I looked. Once again, I was scared and ashamed. I was pregnant by my brother, and I had a sexually transmitted disease. I didn't know much about having an abortion besides the horror stories I saw on TV. I never imagined that I would have to endure the pain, and as usual, no one even asked how I felt. No love for me again.

The doctor didn't put me to sleep for the procedure. He only gave me light anesthesia. I felt all the pain, even though I was assured that I wouldn't feel a thing. That day after we left the clinic, Gina was rather nice to me. She even allowed me to stay in bed all day. We never talked about it, nor did we tell anyone. She told my dad and brothers that it was a female thing. I desperately wanted to tell her what Tim had done to me, but I decided that I would keep it to myself. She probably wouldn't believe me anyway. What I really needed was for my mother to be a mother. Unfortunately, I knew that would not happen, and that hurt deep down inside.

Chapter 3 - A Child is Born

After the experience with my first abortion, I became more of a social butterfly. I had a couple of girlfriends, and "Party" became my middle name. Most of my friends were boys, though. By the time I was thirteen going on fourteen, I had experimented with sex, drugs, and alcohol. I didn't like school anymore, so most of the time I spent it with my friend Keith. He was my best friend, and we occasionally had sex. Keith was not cute at all. He was tall, dark, and ugly. I liked him because he was cool, and nobody messed with me when he was around. Plus, he was sixteen years old, so he had a little more experience than I did. We would spend most of the day smoking weed and drinking. His mom was a dope fiend, and he did not know who his dad was. Therefore, he pretty much did whatever he wanted to do. My dad was a workaholic, and Gina never cared much about what I did anymore. My brothers were in and out the house, so as always I had to fend for myself.

I really did not like Keith as a boyfriend, but he was the closest thing to it until I met Jerome. Jerome was a good guy, and he was cute but very corny. He wasn't the typical "around the way" guy. He got good grades, and he was very active in school. He wanted to do something with his life. On the other hand, I was hopeless, so I really did not care about school or anything dealing with my future, for that matter. He followed me around all the time, and he would do my homework. He loved him some Brea. Jerome would walk me home from school, and believe it or not, Gina thought he was okay. He was two years older than me, but he looked like he could be my age.

I remember being wasted one night at one of the local parties I frequented with Keith. I mean, I had never drank like that before in my life. I recall Keith carrying me out of the party. All I remember was getting to his house, and his big ass sweaty body was all over me. It wasn't sexy at all. I could not move once again, so I just laid there and did nothing. You can say he raped me, but it did not feel like rape. I mean, it was just Keith, and it wasn't like we hadn't had sex before. He was the same guy that I would have given it to if I was sober, so what the hell. This happened a lot, but I never brought it up. It was just the thing to do.

Jerome was very nice, and he never tried to have sex with me. I recall being very seductive with him, just because I knew he would not have sex with me. He would tell me that he was waiting for his wife. I thought he was crazy, because everyone knows that nobody these days waits until they get married. Nonetheless, I did not pressure him until after I found out that I was pregnant for the second time. This time I was a little bit more experienced with knowing about being pregnant. You see, I knew when my period was supposed to come. I also knew that I did not need Gina or any adult to go with me to the doctors, and the visits were free. I absolutely was NOT pregnant by Jerome, because we never had sex. It was Keith's baby for sure. However, Keith was a broke teenager who had no money to help. Hell, he barely had a parent. He was a "stick up kid," but mostly used the money for basic survival like food, water, shelter, and shit like that. Now, Jerome, on the other hand, had a mom and dad that loved him dearly, and they would do anything, *I mean anything* for him.

I remember the first night I forced Jerome to have sex with me. We were at his house, and his parents were not home. I had been touching him all over his body. I knew he was aroused, but he was trying his best not to give in to me. I did not make it easy on him either, and I kind of enjoyed the fact that I was going to be taking advantage of him. The thing was, if I made Jerome have sex with me, I knew his parents would give him the money for me to get my second abortion. Therefore, I decided that day that I had to do what I had to do. I began to pull down his pants and give it to him like I never had before. I saw oral sex on the porn DVDs I had stolen from Ronnie, but I had never done it before. I don't know why, but I actually enjoyed doing it. After I got him good and ready for me, I jumped on top of him, and he came right inside of me. BINGO! That was exactly what I wanted. Once that happened, I knew he would believe me when I told him that I was pregnant by him. Even if he didn't believe me, he would never say a word.

About three weeks later, I told him that I was pregnant by him. Would you know that even though I was only thirteen and he was fifteen, this fool had a nerve to be happy? He was dumber than I thought. I knew there was no way that I was having a baby, so I started crying and telling him how Gina was going to kill me if she found out. I told him I needed the money for an abortion and that he had to get it right away. He was my flunky, so he did exactly what I said. He got the $400 and some change from his dad by giving him some lame excuse. Naturally, his dad believed him. Both of his parents were educators, so they had a nice cushion in the bank. All he had to do was ask.

I knew Gina would catch on after a while, because she knew when my period was supposed to start each month. Well, I got smart. I put ketchup in a pad, so she would think I was on my period. She was so crazy that she would check the bathroom trash to make sure that I came on my period. I think she knew I was pregnant, but she never said anything, and I was glad. By this time, I was having sex with both Keith and Jerome. Jerome had become more into sex. I liked Jerome better than I liked Keith, because he treated me like he loved me. Keith did not treat me bad, but he was just rough and never cared much about how I felt.

The day finally came for me to get the abortion. Jerome was not happy, but he did agree to come with me. We caught a cab to the highly frequented abortion clinic in Cherry Hill. I was so nervous, because I had done this before and knew exactly what to expect. I could see Jerome was very scared, and he did not want me to do it. He was a Christian who had strong faith in God and believed abortion was murder. I don't think the picketers helped with making him feel comfortable. They were screaming bible verses at us and telling us how they could help us. I was creeped out.

He looked at me and said, "Brea, I don't think we should do this."

I assured him that we had no other choice. Once we were inside the clinic, I became a little nervous. You see, I was like Gina in a lot of ways. I cared about what people thought of me. I was a small girl, and I really did look my age, even though I thought I did not at the time. I hated the way the little white college girls were looking at me. We were both doing the same wrong thing, so what the hell were they looking at me for. The time finally came for me to go in the back for the procedure. This time I was put to sleep, so I did not feel any pain. After I was in recovery for a good forty-five minutes, Jerome and I caught a cab back to his house. He took care of me all day, but it would soon be time for me to go home. I felt really bad because not only did I kill a child for the second time, but the baby wasn't even Jerome's yet I made him pay for it. I had used him just like Gina did people. Sadly, I was turning into her at an early age. I was living the life of an adult but had no clue of how bad these childhood decisions would affect my adulthood.

When I got home that night, I was feeling like shit. Of course Gina was on top of it.

"You better not be pregnant, you little whore."

Damn she knew everything, but at the same time, her ass knew nothing.

"Your dad and I can't afford to take care of you and a baby. We work too hard as it is."

I thought to myself, *when the hell did she ever take care of anything or work so hard?* I just brushed her off and told her I was having really bad cramps. I know she didn't believe me, but she left me alone. I had to stop hanging out with Keith, because he was too damn hood. He always wanted to stick somebody up or do grimy shit, even to his own boys. I never told him about the pregnancy. Hell, he wouldn't have cared anyway. I started to spend a lot of time with

Jerome, and he was even allowed to come to my house to do homework. That was kind of cool, because Gina did not even want my one or two home girls to come over. We would have sex right while she was in the house. I did not respect Gina, and no one else was home. She was doped up on pills and alcohol anyway. I started to do what I wanted and began to care less about Gina's thoughts.

When I turned fourteen years old, I started hanging out with an older girl named Tia. She was a senior at the high school on the other side of town. I met her at the mall where she worked. She was cool as hell and very ladylike. She had a pretty face, but she was fat, and she hated being fat. I was a tomboy who wore big baggy clothes. She would tell me how I should dress and that I needed to take a weight gainer because I was too skinny. I began to become obsessed with Tia. She had her own place, because her mom had died from an overdose a year prior. I spent day in and day out with this chick. I thought she was so cool, and I wanted to be like her. She dressed so nice, and she was very popular. She was not from my part of town, but we got along great. She would talk to me about sex and how to please a man. She was the big sister I never had, and I knew Tia loved me. Little did I know, she would turn me into an uncontrollable adult.

Her house was the hang out spot. Sometimes I even went to school with her just to meet boys. We would go to house parties on Freemont Street, and sometimes she would come to my neck of the woods to hit more parties up. Those parties use to bang, even though I was too young to be there. All the fine older guys were there, and I was in heaven. Well, one

night at the regular parties, I met this guy from
Philly. He was so damn sexy, and he had a Lexus.
This was a huge deal for a fourteen year old. Tia had
me all made up, and I had on some tight fitting
clothes. I definitely was not looking my age that
night. He watched me the entire night. Tia even
noticed.

"Girl, you better go get that before I do. He got
a Lex," Tia said as she watched him watching me.

I was scared because this was a man not a
boy. Finally, I stepped up my drinking game and got
the nerve to go over to him. He was looking at me as
if he wanted to just take me right there. By looking at
him, I knew he had to be at least twenty-one. We
started talking, and before I knew it, we were
grinding on the basement wall. I was enjoying myself.
He took control, and I loved it. He would not leave
my side, and I did not want him to neither. He was
Cuban, so he had a little accent, and he was sexy as
hell. He was the most gorgeous man I had laid eyes
on in my life. I was lusting after him.

After the party, I linked up with Tia who was
leaving with some dude as usual. She hopped in
some dude's car and said she would call me
tomorrow, leaving me to walk home alone. I did not
live too far from the party, so it wasn't that bad that
she left me. As I began to walk home, I heard
someone yelling for me to stop. When I turned
around, and it was him. It was Mr. Wonderful.

"What's up, beautiful? What's your name?"

I told him, and he said his name was Vick. He
asked me for my number, but I could not give it to
him because Gina would flip.

He said, "Let me take you home, baby."

I quickly agreed but had him to park down the street, just in case Gina was looking out the window as she often did. She let me do my thing, but she tried to act like she cared. We sat in the car and just talked. Well, he mostly talked, and I hung on to his every word. He was so grown up. He started kissing me and telling me how sexy I was and that he wanted to get to know me a little better. He asked me to go to the motel with him. Even though my heart told me not to, my mind and body said go, so I did.

When we got into the room, he wasted no time giving it to me like no man had ever done. He was caressing my body and making me feel like a complete lady. He took his time, and I loved every bit of it. That night was the first time I had mutual sex, meaning we both wanted it. I didn't care if I was going to get in trouble the next morning. All I could think about was Vick. After he made love to me, he laid me on top of him and whispered in my ear that I was his now. At that moment, it was over for anybody else I was seeing. He had me locked in with those couple of words.

We got up that morning and went to breakfast. After that, he dropped me off home and left his pager number with me. I was floating on cloud nine and had never felt like this before. I could not wait to tell Tia how much he was feelin' me. When I arrived home, Gina did not say much besides the usual "you better not get pregnant" speech and calling me the typical slut and whore that she always called me. I just kept going to my room. My heart was racing. I rushed upstairs to call Tia. She was happy to hear about my night and told me to come over.

I went to Tia's house and gave her every detail.
She told me that I needed to play it cool, because
this wasn't the little boys that I was used to dealing
with. She told me to page him, so I did. He called
right back. He told me to get dressed, because he
was taking me to Atlantic City. It was a Sunday, and
I had school the next day, but I was not passing that
up. I had only been to Atlantic City on family
vacations as a kid. I immediately screamed and told
Tia. She advised me that I needed to be grown up
and act like a lady, not a young girl. She did my hair
and added a couple of pieces for length. Tia coached
me on everything. She told me to make sure I got
drunk, and she handed me a drink she made for me.
She explained that getting drunk always brings the
freak out of everyone. Boy was she right. She put the
finishing touches on my hair and makeup. By the
time she got done, I looked at least eighteen years
old.

That night, he met me at Tia's. I told Gina I
was staying at Tia's. She wasn't cool with it, but she
did not have too much to say. She just said that I'd
better take my ass to school and that Jerome was
calling me all weekend. I had forgotten about the
promotion party for Jerome's dad. He had just
become principal of a suburban school, and they
would be moving after the school year. I was not
worried about Jerome at this time – shit, he would
always be around. When Vick came to get me, he
was lookin' fly as hell, and he smelled so good just
like my daddy use to smell. He had on all the latest
shit including Guess jeans, Polo shirt, and some
fresh Timberland boots. He was rockin' the Philly
uniform at that time. Damn he was fine. When he

looked at me, I knew he was impressed, because I looked and smelled good, too. In no way did I like the little girl that I was. During our drive to Atlantic City, he was complementing me and telling me how sexy I was. He kept telling me that I was his girl. We never talked about age or anything really pertaining to me. All he did was shower me with compliments. When we got there, he took me to a seafood buffet. I noticed that he kept getting up to use the pay phone. It was a little annoying, but I dare not say anything. I was just so happy that my young ass had the opportunity to hang with this man. He was wonderful, and he treated me like I was a grown up. Plus, he had a bunch of money.

After we ate, we went to a nice room at the Howard Johnson. I had only been to the motel with him, so this was a very nice room to me. He immediately undressed me and just stared at my body. I felt a little uncomfortable, because I was so skinny. I was not curvy nor did I have a big ass or big titties. In reality, I was just a little girl. He reached to turn on the light, and I tried to stop him, but he managed to do it anyway. He was just looking at my body in the light, and I was so embarrassed. At that very moment, something inside of me told me that I should not be in this room with this man.

He kissed my body all over and gave me oral sex. He just had my young body turned all out, and he made me lose control. By the time he was done with me, I was telling him that I loved him, and he had talked me into having his child.

He kept saying, "I ain't wear no condom, 'cause you gone have my baby."

I just went right along with it with no resistance. The next morning, I woke up to him arguing with someone on the phone about money and not coming all the way down there to get no profit. I had no clue who it was, and to be perfectly honest, I did not care. I was in love with this man. Finally, I knew what love was. I played sleep, and he woke me up with a kiss and told me we had to go. It was way too late for me to go to school, but I did not care. We really did not talk much on the ride home, and I could sense something was bothering him. To break the silence, I finally asked him his age. He said twenty-five with ease. *Damn, twenty-five? I thought he was like twenty or twenty-one.* If he knew I was fourteen, he probably would have stopped fuckin' with me. So, I lied and told him I was seventeen, and we left it at that. He made a joke about me being jail bait, and I thought nothing of it.

When we arrived at the corner of my house, I told him I loved him and how much I enjoyed our night. He told me he loved me too and that he wasn't going anywhere. Before I got out of his car, he told me that I was his for good. Then, he kissed me, and I went in the house. This time Gina was pissed. I told her that I had overslept, and she went off on me and started calling me names. Although she was putting on her best wild woman performance, it rolled right off my shoulder. You see, I was in love with a man, and he was in love with me. Nothing could change the way I felt, so I thought.

For the next couple of weeks, I had seen Vick almost every day. He was like my god. He bought me things like clothes and always took me out to eat. He was a nice guy. He even asked if he could meet my parents. I told him they were strict and that was out the question. I knew Gina would have a shit fit when she saw him and realized he was eleven years older than me. I had managed to see Jerome once or twice since I started dating Vick. Jerome was a boy, but Vick... Vick was a man, and that was what I needed. About three months into my relationship with Vick, the flames began to die down a little, but we still saw each other and talked every now and then. He had a cell phone by this time, so I could call him directly. Gina even let me get a phone in my room. I was talking to him more than I was seeing him, and I really wanted to see him.

In addition to missing Vick, I had also missed two periods. I was so moody, and I was even snapping back at Gina from time to time. When I got tired of ignoring the facts, I finally went to my infamous place, the Planned Parenthood clinic. At the age of fourteen, I found out that I was pregnant for the third time. I made up my mind that this time was going to be different for sure. I would not have to get an abortion. I was not pregnant by my brother or the nasty boy around the corner. I was pregnant by a man - my man, and he wanted it. Therefore, I could keep the baby, and we would live happily ever after. I soon came to realize that life, especially mine, was no fairy tale.

Tia was the first person that I told, but for some reason, she was not happy. She sat me down and told me that I needed to grow the fuck up and do it fast. She was yelling that Vick was not going to save me. I thought she was just jealous because she never had a guy like Vick, so I just listened. However, I knew once I told Vick I was pregnant, he would be so happy for me. I called him and told him that I needed to talk to him in person right away. He came right over. I walked to the car and told him the good news. He was so happy just like I said. He told me that I could move with him and that he would take care of the baby and me. I was so happy to finally have someone to be there for me. He then told me that I needed to tell my parents, and he wanted to go with me.

As excited as I was about my new connection with Vick, I was too scared to face my parents. First of all, I was only fourteen years old, and Gina would probably kill me for sure. She already hated my guts, and this would definitely take her over the edge. I decided to tell them without Vick and save myself the risk of embarrassment. He took me home after we'd spent most of the day at Tia's home planning our future. I walked in the house ready to spill the beans to Gina and my dad. I called them both downstairs and told them I was pregnant by an older guy. I also let them know that I was moving with him, and I wasn't having an abortion. I was going to keep my baby.

Gina just looked me up and down with disgust, and I could tell that she was pissy drunk.

Surprisingly she said, "Go ahead."

I was thinking, *this is too good to be true.* My dad started to ask me a bunch of questions like *by who* and *how old* and *when did this happen.* I completely tuned him out, because I was so shocked at Gina's reaction. Believe it or not, I wanted her to say something different or get all dramatic like she usually does. I could take it. Where were the sluts and whores that she usually blurted out? All she said was that I would be back and that she would have to take care of a bastard child. I left out the house that day feeling a bit confused, but I was happy.

I ran to Tia's house to call Vick. I paged him and called his cell, but I got no response. I was worried. Even though we never discussed it, I knew he was into something illegal, but I never knew what it was. Finally, he called me back and told me he needed to talk to me in person, and he would meet me at Tia's. He got to Tia's house very late, and I was half-sleep. We sat in his car, so we could have some privacy while we talked. He told me that he was sorry, but he had a live-in girl with two small little girls. However, he still loved me and wanted to be with me, but he could not leave his girls. I started crying uncontrollably. I hadn't cried like that in years. I was so heartbroken. Was he telling me that he was leaving me? Or, was he asking me to get rid of the baby that he said he wanted? That's exactly what he was saying. He had gotten me pregnant even though he had a family.

I told him that I was having the baby, and he would help me. That night, I saw a different side of the quiet, smooth talking man. He cursed me out and called me all the same names Gina would call me. This was the same man who told me that he was happy that I was pregnant with his child, and that he would be there for me. How the fuck did all of that change so fast? What did I do? To make matters worse, the man of my dreams suddenly snapped and punched me directly in my eye! He was like a maniac as he was hitting and chocking me. I was fighting back, but there was no way that I could even land a punch. He was screaming and telling me to stay the fuck away from him and his family and that he wanted nothing else to do with me.

I felt lower than I had ever felt. I knew Gina didn't love me. Hell, no one did, but a piece of me believed that Vick did. I could not believe how he just flipped on me like that. He was acting just like Gina but worse. Was I crazy, or did I have the worst luck in the world when it came to love? He kicked me out of his car and drove off. I wanted to die right there in the parking lot. To top it all off, Tia had witnessed the entire thing. It seems as though she could not wait to rub it in my face. She was so jealous of me for some reason.

She kept saying, "I told you. Man, fuck that nigga. Get the darn abortion, get drunk, and move on."

Some friend she was.

I had a long walk home that day. All I could do was cry. I was always very emotional. He was not going to take me away from my abusive mom. What was I going to do? I had no one to turn to, so I got into Gina mode. I began to plot. I came up with a plan. I would tell Jerome it was his baby again. I mean, I did sleep with him once or twice while I was with Vick, so he would believe me. This way I would get to keep the baby, and no one would know it wasn't Jerome's. I was not getting rid of this baby. I refused. I immediately ran upstairs when I got home and called to tell Jerome it was his. He was so happy, especially when I told him I was keeping it. I told him we would talk it all out the next day, and for the first time, I told him I loved him. LIES. I had no love in my heart for anyone anymore. It was just something to say. I ran downstairs and told Gina that I'd lied about the older guy, and that I was actually pregnant by Jerome. I told her that I didn't want her to hate Jerome and that's why I lied. Once again, she was not upset. Something had to be wrong with her. Was she nuts? I was very nervous. She told me she would handle it, not to worry, and we would discuss it in the morning. What did that mean?

The next morning, I was up bright and early. I went downstairs to make breakfast and walked into Gina, my dad, Jerome, and his parents all discussing the baby. I sat down, and they kept talking like I wasn't there. Jerome was just being quiet. Gina was doing most of the talking. Why wouldn't my dad say anything? Damn, speak up, Dad! She started telling them how crazy I was and that I was not capable of having a child, so she would be taking care of it. They did offer to help. They were the nicest people I've ever met, and they loved their son. They didn't care for me much, because I was a little too advanced for their son. Jerome's dad did most of the talking for their family like a real man, unlike my daddy. When they were done discussing the future of my baby, it was decided that I would keep it, but Gina would have custody and Jerome's parents would pay Gina $100 a week. Gina was something else. She got this all in writing, and that settled it. I was going to have a baby.

Word got around school fast that I was pregnant. Even though everyone knew it was Jerome's baby, they still looked at me funny and whispered behind my back. Some of the girls that I was cool with informed me that their parents didn't want them to have any interaction with me, even though some of those girls were the biggest hoes. It bothered me but not so much. I was just worried about bringing this baby into the world when I was still a baby myself. Everywhere we went, adults and teenagers alike were asking me how old I was and why would I want a baby. I remember when we went to find out what we were having. The nurses where whispering, but I could hear every word they were saying. My age was so much of a concern to them. The doctor came in and told Jerome, Gina, and me that it was a boy. Gina and I said, "Thank God" at the same time. I knew she would treat him right, because she liked boys and hated girls. Then again, maybe she just hated me.

The doctor turned to me and said, "Young lady, you need to keep your legs closed and not get pregnant. You're going to be a fifteen year old mom."

Gina shook her head and began to tell the doctor how she tried everything with me but I never listened and how I came from an amazing home. The doctor and Gina left the room to continue discussing how horrible I was. Jerome tried to console me. I guess he could see the pain in my eyes. However, my pain was so much deeper than being pregnant at fourteen and a mom at fifteen. It was more of the abuse that I had endured at the hands of everyone. Either everyone used me, or I used them. I often wished Tim would have killed me instead of killing himself.

After nine months of a pretty decent pregnancy, my water broke, and we all rushed to the hospital. Even Ronnie and Mark were there. Gina was doing all the talking, and my dad was right by my side holding my hand. He kept telling me everything was going to be okay. I wanted to believe him, but nothing in my life was ever okay. I just wished everyone would be quiet and leave the room. I just wanted silence. In the back of my mind, I wished Vick was there and secretly hoped that he would one day change his mind. Tia, who I barely talked to anymore, said she heard he got locked up for drugs, but I never heard anything else about him after that.

I had a natural child birth, and it was literally the worst physical pain I had ever felt. After about an hour of pushing, a beautiful baby boy with so much hair was born. He looked just like Vick. Damn, they were twins. Nobody said anything, and Jerome's parents started praying.

Meanwhile, Ronnie whispered in my ear, "Girl, he don't look like Jerome at all."

He kind of looked like me, so it wasn't as bad as Ronnie made it seem. Besides, I knew he wasn't Jerome's baby, so his looks were no surprise to me. It was a beautiful experience, I guess, but I was just glad that I wasn't pregnant anymore. Gina was the first person to hold him, of course. We decided to name him Jerome, Jr. It was the easiest, and I really did not care what we named him. I wasn't interested in any of this until the time came for me to hold him, and I got very emotional. The moment I laid eyes on my son, I fell in love with him. I didn't think I would, but I loved him. I finally had something that was mine, because he came from me. As the tears of joy streamed down my cheeks, it suddenly dawned on me that I had signed custody over to Gina. Therefore, he really wasn't mine after all. That damn Gina won again. She sure had a way of controlling everyone around her, including my son and me. However, that custody crap didn't matter to me, because he was still my son. I was going to do right by him, so when I got old enough, I could take him away from Gina and all the craziness that came with my life.

Chapter 4 - All Grown Up

After I had my son, I grew up, and I mean I
grew up fast. I realized that there was no time to be a
scared little girl anymore. I couldn't worry about
what happened to me in the past, because no one
cared. Jerome was a senior, and he was doing very
well in school. He was talking about going to Yale or
Harvard. This nigga was smart, and he loved his son.
He always talked about marrying me, but I knew it
was not going to happen. I just wanted to graduate,
so I could get Rome aka Jerome, Jr. out of Gina's
house and move far away from New Jersey. Ever
since I had the baby, she was obsessed with him. He
became her life. She acted like no one could touch
him. She cared for him during the day and refused to
let us put him in daycare. Jerome's parents had
agreed to pay for a good private daycare, but Gina
was not having it. It really did not matter to me as
long as I could go to school.

By this time, I cared about my education
because the baby and I could not live with Gina for
much longer. Jerome talked his dad into letting me
use their address so I could go to school with him in
his part of town. The education was much better
than the one I was getting. I guess you could say
Jerome was my boyfriend, but I never acknowledged
it. When I went to school in the 'burbs, I came to a
lot of realizations. White people had just as many
issues as black folk - different issues, but issue
nonetheless. Every Friday, they brought the dogs in
to search lockers for drugs. I even saw some white
chicks snorting cocaine in the bathroom. I ain't never
see no shit like that at the high school in the hood. I

mean, niggas smoked weed and drank, but that cocaine shit was for the birds. I finally realized what Gina had been trying to say about white people. They were just as screwed up as black people. It just wasn't publicized on the news so much, since they kept their issues in the closet.

I was finally meeting new people, and I had definitely become a little lady at this point. I was still very skinny, but I had way more curves, and the boys at school noticed. None of them interested me, but I was the world's biggest flirt. Toward the end of the year, I met a new guy named P. He was twenty-one and lived with his mom not too far from Jerome. He was cute but a little corny to me. He wore Reeboks and shit. Ain't no nigga in the hood wear them since they stopped making the different color ones. His gear was not up, but he did have a nice car, and I knew I could take him.

Since I had Rome, Gina did not do much for me at all. My dad would slide me money here and there, but he really did not have it like he did in the past. No one bought me clothes anymore, they only helped out with Rome. He got everything, and that damn kid was so spoiled. Gina would always say if I never got pregnant she wouldn't have another mouth to feed. Not only was my daddy taking care of Rome, but Jerome parents paid Gina $100 a week as promised and bought him everything a kid could ever want. I remember they bought him a train that went around the track like on Silver Spoons his first Christmas. I thought it was all a little too much.

Jerome wasn't really giving me too much either, so I had to get a new flunky and that was P. Jerome was so focused on school, but I needed shit and had to make something happen. P was cool, and we had started smoking weed at the park and busting it up. It would not be long before I would seduce him into falling in love with me. It was not hard at all. The black chicks we went to school with were corny as hell, and I had that city swag. Besides, those chicks all had slept with the same guys over and over and traded boyfriends. P would pick me up from school and take me home every day. He worked, but he was a straight momma's boy. They had a couple dollars since his dad had died. He was in the military or some shit, so they had some money put up. He probably would never leave his momma's house. Typical.

P was not my man, even though he thought he was. Jerome was so jealous, but he was not my man either. So what could he do besides be jealous? I was sixteen, and I knew about the world, so I thought. I would always talk to P about getting out of New Jersey because wasn't shit there. I told him how I wanted to get my own spot and how I needed money and shit. He always told me that he could make some shit happen for me because he loved me so much. Most of the time I just ignored what he was saying, because he was a bullshitter - all talk no action. He talked that tough guy talk, but if I would have brought his ass to the hood, he would have got took for everything he had. I wanted to set the boy up, but I was not that mean back then. I was getting there, but I still had that little girl in me.

One day I got into a really bad argument with Gina - I mean really bad. She always tried to control me with Rome. I was decent mom, you know, but I wasn't real loving and shit. Like, we didn't kiss and hug, but he knew I loved him. At this time, I wasn't going to the club like that, so I barely did anything without Rome. When I got money from P for me, I would buy Rome the latest. He had every Jordan, and he kept a fresh haircut. I wasn't getting any real money because I was still young, but I knew I needed to move and fast. Gina was becoming very neurotic. She was doing shit like spending the bill money that my dad had worked so hard to get and then acting as if it was everyone else's fault. I didn't want Rome around her stupid ass at all.

P probably got sick of me telling him how much I wanted to get out of Gina's house. One day he told me about his Uncle Al who had some rental property available. I begged P to call his uncle with a sob story about me so I could rent a place from him. His uncle said he was not about to let some teenage girl stay in his house. He was a devout Christian man, and he did not agree with doing that. I talked P in letting me speak to his uncle. Shit, I was desperate. After our brief conversation, he agreed to meet me at the local grocery store to further discuss what he could do for me, if anything. He picked me up, and to my surprise, he was not a very old man as I had imagined. As a matter of fact, he was rather young and sexy as ever. He was a smooth man. Gina would have said he was a cat daddy - whatever that meant. He reminded me of how my daddy was when he was a young man. Whatever you wanted to call him, I was on it.

On the drive to the small one bedroom apartment he had for rent, he asked me to tell him about my situation. I basically told him a whole bunch of bullshit to get him off my back and make him feel sorry for me. I had a fucked up life so far, but I wasn't going to tell him that. I just told him my mom put me out. As Gina would say, what happens in this house stays in this house. When we got to the apartment, I could tell it was shabby. Still, it wasn't Gina's house, so it was good enough for me. Anything would have been good enough back then. As we walked inside, my back was to him while I was asking questions about cost. I could feel him staring at me.

He quickly responded, "It depends."

I snapped back, "Depends on what?"

As I looked into his eyes, it hit me that this nigga was one of those fake Christians that professed his love of God while cheating on his wife, drinking, and looking at every young girl's ass that walked pass. I knew the type. He was just another dirty old man that would give me what I needed if I gave him some ass. In my heart, I was not feeling this situation at all, but I figured it could be worse.

I went into hustle mode as I walked up to him and took control of the situation. We had sex all over that apartment. Even though I really hated having sex, I knew it could get me what I needed at the time. So, I just went to another place mentally when it was time to have sex with anyone. To be honest, I did like the fact that sex gave me power, because I was just a broken little girl without it. I was about to get what I wanted, and I knew it. He was turned out. By the time we left, I had the keys to the apartment. He told me not to worry about the rent, and we could discuss it later. I made it clear to this dirty old man that I was discreet, so he didn't need to tell P or anyone else of our arrangement. I told him that he was an old man and could get into a lot of trouble for messing with me. He just shook his head in disbelief. I know he thought I was crazy, and I was. I was becoming a major manipulator, and I got a kick out of it. My mind began to wander out of control, I enjoyed making people be fools for me.

When I moved to the new place two weeks later, Gina was not happy. She didn't care that I was leaving, she just didn't want me to take her precious Rome from her. She was so fucking pitiful, and I enjoyed making her suffer. There was no way I was going to get Rome full-time. I just liked to act like I would one day. The older she got, the sadder she became. It was so funny to see her suffering, but she was still an evil bitch. After all the shit I had been through, my personality was very vindictive. I never knew love, so I wasn't showing nobody love - not even my own child. I used to always say I did it all for him, but looking back, it was more for my self-satisfaction. I was addicted to fucking people over.

After I moved in, P thought he was going to stay there as well. I knew how to nip that in the bud. I told his uncle, and he strongly advised P that he would not have us fornicating in his house - even though his married, holier than thou ass was in my bed every other night. I liked P to come over but on my terms. By this time, I was seeing a few other guys. I did not pay rent, but I still had to pay other bills and I wasn't working at the time, so I needed them for something. My daddy who would give me the world was being sucked dry by Gina, so he did as much as he could without her knowing. I was having unprotected sex with the three to four guys I was sleeping with plus P and his uncle. On top of that, every now and then I would have sex with Jerome. Back then, I never used a condom. I mean *never.*

I had become a heavy drinker, and I barely went to school but somehow maintained a C average, so it was all good. My apartment was actually pretty nice, but I barely had Rome. I was too busy drinking and having sex with all kinds of boys and men that Rome did not need to be around. Generally, he stayed with Gina. Sometimes it was annoying, because she never wanted him to spend time with me, but it was cool since he wanted to stay with her all the time anyway.

P would often come over, and he began to talk like he was in love with me and that we were going to be moving really soon. I would always play the good girl role like I wanted to be with him, but truth be told, I did not even like him like that. I mean he was okay, but he didn't give me that feeling like the one I had when I first met Vick. He was so corny, and he was a sucker. I hated that. He reminded me of how my dad was with Gina. He would tell me that he would do anything for me and that he had something in the works. I would just say "Ok, baby," but in the back of my mind, I was laughing like *WE ain't doing shit together.* On top of all this, Uncle Al was becoming more and more aggressive regarding my relationship with P. He was telling me to break it off and that he was leaving his wife. They both were driving me crazy. I had to get rid of one or both of them, and I had to do it fast.

Toward the end of my junior year, P started getting a lot of money. I never asked him how he got it. I just assumed his mommy was looking out for him. Well, I was wrong. One night after drinking, smoking, and unsafe sex, P confided in me that he was making runs with his cousin to Virginia. He was the getaway driver in a bunch of bank robberies, and he was telling me how easy it was. He also told me about some check scheme he was doing. Ole boy was getting it, and I had no clue. To most of the guys I messed with, I may have seemed gullible or naïve, but you best believe I was taking it all in on the low. I talked P into leaving the money with me so his mom wouldn't get suspicious. He agreed to it without hesitation. He was bank robbing every weekend, then dropping his portion off at my house. I was taking him for his money little bit by little bit. He never noticed, or if he did, he just didn't care. Dude was doing it so big that it had become local news. The police were clueless, but the FBI was involved, so shit became heated.

I started hanging out a lot that summer. I was in the twenty-one and older club over in Philly, and I enjoyed the casinos in Atlantic City. I was hanging with P more since he was becoming the man, even though I still didn't look at him as my man. I kind of groomed him into a fly ass dude. I got my sense of style from Gina, and the more money I had, the more I had to shop. I barely went to school; instead I went on shopping sprees courtesy of P's money. We were laundering money in the Atlantic City casinos. At the time, I had no clue about any of that shit. I was just happy to be having my own money to spend and not having to beg Gina or sneak it from my dad.

Not too much later, shit started to get hot. It got so hot that there was a $50,000 reward out for these niggas. At the time, that was a shit load of money. I had been hitting Gina off, but she became suspicious. She accused me of being a stripper and asking where was I getting the money from all of a sudden. I didn't pay her any attention until one day my mind was plotting. I was getting sick of having P around. He was blocking my flow from other guys, and I needed the cash flow that he was not giving me. First, I thought about taking the $150,000 he had stashed at my house and just leaving the state and never looking back. That wasn't going to work, since I was only seventeen years old and I could only go so far.

While I was at Gina's house one day, I confided in her about what was going on with P and his cousin. I even told her about the reward and that I had $150,000 in my possession. I don't know what the fuck I was thinking. I guess I just needed to tell someone, and I had no girlfriends since Tia had moved to Cali with someone's husband. Needless to say, this was another big mistake in my long list of fuck-ups. Just as soon as I left the house, this bitch was calling the damn tip line and saying that my boyfriend and I were the ones robbing banks in VA. The next day, I was at my house with P when the fucking FBI showed up with a warrant and turned my house upside down. Rome was not there, it still was so humiliating. All I kept thinking was *I know this bitch, my so called mother, did not do this to me.*

As P and I sat on my green leather sofa while the investigators did their job, guess who walks through the door? Gina. She brought her ass in there crying, "God, please don't let them take my baby, my only daughter. She is too young to go to jail." I was thinking, *she cannot be talking about me. I know her ass turned us in, and she enjoyed every bit of it.* My dad was there as well. This once powerful man was just standing there like a pussy helping her up, as she went through her dramatic spell. She was so good that they called the ambulance to make sure she was okay.

All P said in a faint whisper was, "Baby, it's gonna be okay. Don't tell them shit."

I felt sorry for him for a split second, but then I snapped out of it. Hell, I knew everything was going to be okay, because I wasn't going to jail for nobody. They collected all the evidence, and took us to the station. It seemed that everyone including my dad was worried about Gina. Rome was still small, so he enjoyed all the excitement. At the time, I thought I was a bad mom, too. I knew I was a bad person, but overall I thought I was a decent mom until I started fucking up.

When we got to the station, I was interrogated for many hours. So far, the seventeen years I'd been on earth were bullshit, and I was a piece of shit. I began to think about Gina and how much she fucked me up. I couldn't fuck Rome up like that. I thought about Jerome getting Rome if I went to jail. Then, the thought of Gina getting him full-time was too much for me to handle. In my mind, I knew I was not going to jail. If I had to screw the entire fucking judicial system, so be it. There was no way in hell, she could have him. Her delusional ass would definitely turn him against me. He was all I really had, even though I wasn't the best mom.

As I thought about what would happen to my son, they asked me the same questions over and over again, but I didn't say shit. I remembered some shit about pleading the fifth and that's exactly what I did.

After ten to twelve hours in there, I was finally going home. Come to find out, P had confessed and said that I had nothing to do with it. That was cool and crazy at the same time. I told my psycho mom, and she turned him - well us in, but he did not want me to suffer, so he just confessed. Damn, he must have really cared about me even though I really didn't give a fuck about him. Honestly, I really didn't know how to give a fuck about anything, since no one really gave a fuck about me.

When I was ready to leave the station, no one from my family was there, so my stupid ass called Gina and my daddy.

My dad said, "You really have your mom upset, and she can't talk right now, Baby. I have to stay with her, so catch a cab here, and I'll pay for it."

That was all he had for me after I was just interrogated for hours. He really didn't love me like I thought he did, but he surely loved Gina. He was such a fool for her! There was no way he was *that* in love with her. What did she have over this man? Rather than figure that shit out, I called Jerome but forgot he was away at some function trying to better his life. All the men I was dealing with were all too busy. How convenient. When they needed some pussy, I was there. All I needed was a ride home, so I called my last resort, Uncle AL's nasty perverted ass who had become obsessed with my tender ass. He came immediately.

Before he got there, I could not stop throwing up. The thought of him made me sick. He had this odd smell like he did not wash his dick, ever. All I could think was, *I am not sucking his dick. Not today.* I got in the car, and he looked happy to see me. The feeling was not mutual. He took me to my place and invited himself in like his old ass was my damn man. I was never mean to guys, so I just went with the flow. To add to the already hectic events of the day, he just kinda pushed me in the door and started screaming shit like "slut, whore, and bitch." He turned crazy like everyone else in my life did. He called himself chastising me for behaving badly. He said that I was sure to burn in hell, because God does not like sinners like me.

He accused me of dropping the dime on his nephew and said he was going to get revenge. How did he know what his nephew had done? P said he only told me and no one else. He wanted to get revenge, but for me, just being around him was revenge enough. I was clever, so I flipped it on him so quick. I fell to my knees and begged.

"Please, baby! I love you. Don't do this to me. I'm so sorry!"

He was really stunned as he just stood there looking at me. Hell, my act was really working, because his old ass damn near looked like he wanted to cry with me. I really laid it on thick as I began to cry, and I mean *really cry*. I had learned from the best. Gina was great at getting people to feel sorry for her, and I was about use her shit to my advantage. He picked me up from the floor and carried me to the bed. I let him fuck me and acted as if it was the best, as I often did with guys. He was taking it all in like he was really putting it down. Finally, he climaxed and dozed off.

I did not sleep much that night. All I could think about was P, Rome, Gina, how fucked up my life was, and how I really wished I was dead. I was

hopeless and depressed. Then, a light bulb went off
in my head. The feds never said anything about the
$150k that I stashed for P. Wait a minute. They must
have found it, RIGHT? I got up slowly, hoping not to
wake up Uncle Al. I went into the living room,
pushed that green leather sofa to the side, and
pulled up the floor board. OH MY GOD! Every penny
of it was there. I could not believe they had actually
missed the money. What was I going to do? I thought
to myself, *this could be my way out.*

At that moment, my whole life flashed before
me. All that I had endured up until then would be
over. I was rich - well not rich, but it was a hell of a
start. I put the sofa back and eased back in the bed,
trying not to disturb the dirty old man. He woke up,
put his clothes on, and left without saying a word. I
should have known that was odd, because he always
had so much to say. For the next few days, I just
plotted what I should do. Should I go to Cali with
Tia? I mean, she was the only female friend I had.
Maybe I should go to Delaware or Hotlanta? Damn,
how was I going to pull this off?

P had been calling collect ever since he got
locked up, but I didn't answer. I didn't want him to
ask about the money. I didn't even know if he knew
that they didn't take the money, and I didn't want to
know. I acted normal by going to school here and
there. I was dipping in the money but not really
spending a lot. I finally decided that I was going to
Atlanta. I was going to pay cash for one years' worth
of rent, but I could just go to a hotel until I could
find a place. I would just leave Rome with Gina until
I got situated. I would get my GED, and then go to
hair school and maybe open my own shop.

One thing I always knew how to do was hair. Yep, I had it all figured out. I wasn't going to tell anybody. I would just go, and I could call Gina once I got situated.

Uncle AL hadn't really been bothering me much since our last encounter, and I was so glad, because I really hated being around him. I mean, he was the worst kind of man being married and sleeping with a young girl and God knows who else. So a few days before I was scheduled to leave, I had decided that I was going to just pack my clothes and catch the Greyhound to the ATL. I was so hype because this would give me a chance to finally have a real life. No one knew me in Atlanta, so I could start fresh. I rushed home after leaving Gina's that night and began to pack all the clothes that I had. I bought my bus ticket and was set to leave the next morning. I had never been happier. I moved the green leather sofa to get the money, so I could stash it safely for the long ride to Georgia. Would you know nothing was there? I mean nothing. No money at all.

I started to lose control of my breathing, and that old feeling came back on me. I was having a panic attack. I told myself to calm down and maybe I had moved it. I searched that small eight hundred square foot apartment high and low. What the fuck? It was just there a few days ago! There was no way this was really happening. No one knew about the money besides P and me, so how could it be gone? Suddenly I remembered that Uncle AL was at the apartment the night I discovered the money. But, he was sleep, so there was no way he knew what I had found. He couldn't have... or could he? FUCK. What was I going to do? I decided to call him and see if he would come over. I couldn't ask him right out about the money, but he had to have it since no one else had access to the apartment, not even Gina.

I called him all night until he finally came over just around 2 a.m. He was acting very suspicious, and I couldn't help but just come right out and ask his ass.

"Did you take the money, AL? Did you?!"

He stood there looking as if he had no clue at what I meant.

Eventually, he said, "Brea, how would someone get away with taking that much money?"

I knew then that he took it, because I never said how much it was. All I said was that I was missing some money. I immediately started hitting him and demanding that he give me the money. I was hysterical. I saw all my dreams of moving out of state, having my own salon, and being a good mom to Rome all go down the drain. He was trying to stop me from kicking his ass, but I couldn't control myself. I needed that money. He finally ended up restraining me and told me that he did not take any money. Then, he said that I needed to be out by the next day or he would call the police and say I was trespassing. I never signed a lease, so I thought he could just put me out. I was begging and crying for him to just give me the money or even give me half of it. He stepped over me and headed out the door while I was on the floor in devastation.

After he stormed out, I remember getting on my knees and asking God why He made my life so hard and if I could just catch a break. I was only seventeen yet I had lived the life of about three adults. I just wanted peace of mind. On top of that, I would have to go back to Gina's house. Why couldn't somebody just love me enough to save me? There was nothing I could do about my situation. Who the hell could I tell that my boyfriend's uncle that I was having sex with stole the stash that I had from my boyfriend's robberies? I was so fucked.

The next day, I went to Gina's to talk to my dad. He instantly knew something was wrong.

He asked, "Anything I can help you with?"

I wanted to say, *yes be my dad, leave Gina, and take me away from this madness.* This was the first but not the last time that I seriously considered contemplating suicide. I just told him no and asked if I could come back home because I missed them and it was too hard living on my own. He immediately said yes. He had so much pain in his eyes. He always looked like he needed a hug. I always felt sorry for him because Gina had him under a spell. The power of the P U S S Y. After our brief talk, he took me to get my things, and I moved back into the room that I spent most of my days and nights in over the years. Life would never get better. P stopped calling. I guess he got the point. I always thought of writing him, but I just didn't know what to say. I mean, he was cool and all, but he was going to be in jail for a long time, so there's no point in me caring. I never heard from Uncle AL again, but if I ever got my hands on him, he would regret it.

Chapter 5 - I's Married Now

After moving back in with Gina, I managed to graduate from high school and was even going to hair school. I was trying to be a better me despite constantly being called a failure, low life, and whore in front of my son by the woman who gave birth to me. I was actually used to the abuse, since I had endured it for so long. By this time, I was nineteen and things were fine. Mark had gotten married and lived with his wife and kids. He was actually doing all right as well. Ronnie was going by "Rhonda" and had moved to the mecca for gay black people, ATLANTA, GA. Gina hated that he had turned into Rhonda, but I actually liked it. I finally had a big sister to look up to. Daddy was still working, but he was getting his social security check and working part time as a handy man. Gina still went from A to Z without warning. Rome always wanted Gina, and he never really liked me. I was like his big sister. He loved her so much, and she loved him, too. I could never understand why she didn't love me like she loved him. Nonetheless, things were looking up for me.

I would go clubbing with a few girls from around the way, but I mainly hung out with my cousin Draya. She was cool as hell, and she was so damn confident. She was two years older than I was and she always had the latest trends. She had a baby by a big time drug dealer who was married but he helped her out and bought her and her son whatever they wanted. She was small like me, so she would give me her hand-me-downs, but they were still practically new. She was Gina's sister's daughter, but Gina never liked her. Gina never really liked anybody. Things quickly shifted.

I was hanging with Draya every day and I pretty much lived with her. She had a nice condo, and I can't lie, I was so jealous and I wanted to live like that. She had the nicest two-door BMW that her baby daddy bought for her. I just had the Honda Civic that Mark left for me when I graduated. She and I would lay in the bed and just talk about everything, but I never told her any of my dark secrets - especially about what Tim had done to me. We never really talked about me. It was mostly about her, how she loved her baby's daddy, and how he was going to leave his wife. I believed every word she said.

She would tell me how good he was in bed and that he had the biggest dick ever. I never really liked sex, so that part never interested me. I just loved the way he treated her. It seemed like he really loved her even though he was married. He used to come and spend the night over all the time. His wife even knew about Draya but would not allow her son over to their house. Draya and I became so close that she convinced me to move in with her. I slept on the sofa most of the time. Rome and her son were the same age, so they played together all the time. All we did was get drunk and party. She would have card games at her house all the time.

I met a guy named Gene at one of those parties. He was not my type at all. He was short, dark-skinned, and ugly like my dad. I liked my men tall, light-skinned, and cute pretty boys. He did dress very nice, and he hit on me the whole night. He had money, so Draya told me to stop looking on the outside. I gave him a chance. He ended up staying that night after the party. To my surprise, he was very nice, and he did not try to have sex with me. Most of the guys I knew, would always tell me how sexy I was. He kept saying how pretty I was, and I think I was blushing. He didn't give me butterflies yet, but this was a start. We talked all night. He talked about himself a lot and told me that he was going to be a producer. He was honest enough to tell me that he was a small time drug dealer under Draya's baby's dad Mike. However, he was trying to focus solely on his music, but he had three kids by the same girl.

Gene was a few years older than I was, but he was a little immature. He made me laugh a lot, and he was never serious. After that night, he began to come over with Mike almost every day. He took me on a few dates, and I really enjoyed his company. He was so much fun. After about two weeks of dating him, the time came for us to have sex. We made love right on sofa, and it was good but different. I was not always present during sex because I didn't really like it, but I felt a strong connection to him after this. He kept making sure I was okay, and he was kissing me and taking his time. It was refreshing to have someone really take time with me. I think I was falling in love.

Things were great after about a month of dating. The only thing that was odd was that he never stayed the night with me. He always left in the middle of the night, but I was his girl and needed to understand that hustling was his job. Draya was very happy for me. She was my biggest supporter. I hadn't had anybody show me so much genuine love since Tim. We would see how that turned out, since I always had my guard up. I told my dad and Gina about him, because I wanted them to see how much someone loved me.

Gina just said, "Brea, you are so stupid. That man don't love you. He don't even know you."

Why couldn't she just be happy for me? Why was it so hard for her to believe that someone loved me? My daddy did say he was happy for me, and he wanted to meet him. Gina made it clear that she could care less about some man that was into me, and he wasn't allowed in her house. Daddy took up for me, and for some reason, Gina didn't argue with him. She agreed to have him over for Sunday dinner.

When I told Gene, he was so excited. I finally had someone that loved me. He even hung out with Rome a little bit. By this, time Jerome was not home as often. He was in Central Jersey at Princeton, but he always spent time with Rome when he did come home. He stopped having sex with me about a year prior. It didn't really bother me, especially now that I had a man. We went to Gina's house for Sunday dinner. Daddy had made a spread, and Mark and his family came. It was like a real family. Gina was even acting very nice, and she seemed to like him.

"Ms. Gina, I really love your daughter, and I want to marry her," Gene said, catching us all by surprise.

My mouth hit the floor. We had only been dating a few months, and we never talked about getting married. She took him into the kitchen and told me to stay in the living room. I was so nervous, and I didn't know what to do or what was she telling him. Knowing her, she was probably telling him that

I was crazy. All I could think was that she better not fuck it up for me. They finally came out and everything seemed normal. Everybody seemed to like him.

As we drove back to Draya's place, he stopped the car and looked me in the eyes.

"I love you, Brea, and I don't care about anything in your past. You can share anything with me. Let's get married."

I was stunned again, because we had never talked about any of this or my past. I didn't ask him what she said when they were alone. I simply said okay. And, just like that, we were getting married. It wasn't a down on one knee proposal like I saw on the TV shows. No ring. Nothing. However, he really loved me if he wanted to marry me, right?

I was working at a local hair salon making reasonable money, but I was just a shampoo girl, so I was making mostly tips. We moved in together about a week after he "proposed." We had a room for his two daughters and a room for Rome and his son. We had our own family. I didn't know much about him, and I had never seen his baby's mom or met his mother. It was kind of weird, but I did not read too much into it. Every time his phone would ring, he would leave the room to talk on it. It didn't bother me because daddy did that a lot, too, and there was no way he was cheating on Gina. We decided to have a shotgun wedding at the courthouse since he expressed that he did not have much family and he just wanted to be married to me.

I was only twenty, and I had no idea why I was getting married. I had only known him a few months, but the love was there for sure. His kids never came over the house to spend the night, and we mainly did things together. Rome was usually with Gina because he was a cry baby, and he would tell Gina everything. We decided that only Mike and Draya would come with us. He didn't have a lot of money like Mike, but he did manage to get me a small one carat diamond cluster. It wasn't what I dreamed of as a child while lying in my beautiful canopy bed, but I thought it would do. I was content.

I wore a small little white dress, and he wore a black and white linen outfit. It was as nice as it could have been for the crowded Camden County courthouse. He was seeing everybody he knew. I knew a lot of people by face, but no one really liked me because of the rumors they'd heard about me. He was popular as hell, and Mike was the man in the city. People kept on stopping us and saying congratulations while we were waiting in the long line to get married. He seemed very uncomfortable, but he didn't say anything. He kept checking his phone. We finally got married after an hour long wait. The wedding lasted four minutes. It was nothing like I imagined. We went to Red Lobster right after that and then we just went home. He ripped my clothes off as soon as we got home and had sex with me right in the doorway. It was so fast. He left right after, and things just didn't feel right. I did feel like I loved him, but I also felt like something was not right and that I had made a big mistake. I did not tell Gina or my dad, because I knew they would have something negative to say - especially Gina. I just sat alone on my wedding day thinking about how I got to that point. Somehow, I thought that getting married would one day make me happy, but that wasn't quite the case.

The next few months were awkward to say the least. He only stayed home every now and then, and he was making excuses like he had to go to the studio. I still hadn't told Gina that I was married, because I just didn't want to hear what she had to say. Draya and I were still hanging out but not as much. She was my best friend. One night, Gene came home pissy drunk, which was something he rarely did. He wasn't a big drinker, you know. Therefore, something in me was suspicious. You can even say I was nosey. I started going through his pockets. I really don't know what I was looking for. I came across his cell phone. I was not the one to really pry, but I could not help myself. I opened the phone and saw multiple calls from the same one number, and he had a few voicemails. Something told me not to check, but I could feel myself getting anxious as I often did. I made a quick decision to check the voicemail. I mean there was no passcode or anything on it.

I listened to the voicemail, and I could hear a lady screaming, "Why the fuck you ain't come home?! I'm sick of this shit, and come get your damn kids!"

This had to be his baby's mom, Kia. I had never seen her, but I had heard her voice. Draya told me that she met her once or twice, but she didn't really know her like that. He would drop his kids off, but he would always park at the corner and then walk up. Looking back, I guess that was weird that I never met her considering I was married to the father of her kids. Why was she on his voicemail asking him to come home when our place was his home? I wanted to wake him up right then and there, but something told me to wait. I went through all the messages until the sun came up. I was confused by what I saw. They had multiple messages about being in love, getting married, and how she may be pregnant again. What the fuck was going on? I just laid there in tears. Once again, I was so hurt. I knew something was funny, but I didn't think he was still seeing her of all people. He told me he couldn't stand her and that she was a bitch which was why he didn't want me to meet her. All those things were going through my head. I was going to confront him, but first I needed to tell Draya.

I acted normal when he got up the next day. I was good at acting like everything was cool. I had been doing that my whole life.

"I'm sorry I came in drunk last night, Babe. Tonight, I'm gonna take you somewhere special, so be ready about eight o'clock. Love you, boo," he said as he gave me a kiss before heading out the door.

Babe, boo, love. Those were all the same words he used in the many messages with Kia. It was clear that he didn't love me. I just said okay as he walked out the door. Right after that, I went straight to Draya's house. She was home drinking as usual, and Mike was leaving as I was coming. He never really spoke to me, and he was a little rude to me. I had no clue why because I never did anything to him. When he left, I told Draya the whole story with tears and spit coming from my mouth. I was devastated. He was cheating on me.

"Brea, calm down. He's just being a man."

What was she saying? Why was it okay for him to do this to me? This shit just didn't feel right. I knew I had been through a lot, but Gene was always so nice to me. He loved me. Even though I hadn't known him long, he was never mean to me.

She basically told me to stop looking for shit, because I was going to find it. That was the stupidest shit I had ever heard. The reason I was looking was to see what I could find. I just listened to her brush my problems off as she talked about herself. She talked about how Mike was really leaving his wife and that he had been staying at her house all week. That shit was not sitting well with me. Why would she sit and have a whole conversation about her cheating with a married man when that was what I was going through? I didn't say shit. I never said shit. I had no real voice, but I was going to say something to Gene at dinner. I left to go pick Rome up from school and drop him off at Gina's. I didn't have time to talk to Daddy like I usually did when I dropped Rome off. I went to the mall to get something sexy to wear. I stopped in Victoria's Secret to get the sexiest thongs and bra I could find. I was not very sexual, but I was very sexy as I was often told by the many men that I came across. I found a cute dress to wear. If he wanted Kia, he wouldn't want her anymore after seeing me.

I got home just in time to take a nice long shower and get dressed. All I could think about was why he lied to me. He still wanted her, but he married me. I was even more confused. I drunk half of the bottle of Hennessey we had in the house to calm my nerves. He came in around eight-thirty that evening. He kissed me and jumped in the shower. We went to a nice restaurant with a name that I couldn't pronounce. The food was amazing, and he knew I loved Italian food. I was already drunk and the dinner was going great. We were playing with each other at the table, and things were going great until we got in the car. I just had to open my big mouth.

"Gene, does Kia know we got married?"

He looked annoyed, "No, Brea. She doesn't know yet, just like your mom and dad don't know. It's complicated."

"Complicated? What the fuck is so complicated about being in love and married? Huh?"

He didn't say shit. He just started the car and began driving home. I was determined to get my answers.

"Pull over, Gene. Pull the muthafuckin car over now."

"Cool out, Brea, damn. I got shit in the car, and you acting stupid. We'll talk about it when we get home."

I went on and on about all the stuff I saw in his phone. He did not say a word, and that pissed me off even more. I was drunk, so I was going a mile a minute. If I wasn't drunk, I wouldn't have said a word.

When we got in the house, he walked ahead of me and started up the long spiral steps to the bedroom. I was on his heels. In that second, he turned around and kicked the shit out of me down about thirteen steps, and I hit my head on the wall.

"Shut the fuck up, you stupid ass bitch! Your mom said you was a crazy bitch! Damn, all you do is bitch."

My heart dropped the same way it had when Tim turned on me in the basement and when Vick told me he didn't want me and he had another family. I cried silently and picked myself up. I went into Rome's room and cried myself to sleep. I woke up to the smell of his cologne and him kissing me and apologizing. Then he left me alone to cry and console myself. It was still dark outside, so I had no idea where he was going. I was so fucked up in the head that I was questioning myself. Why did I have to search his phone when things were going fine? Why did I feel so guilty like I was the one who did something wrong? I just wished I had someone who I could really talk to like a normal mom. I knew I could call Draya, but it was late. I just laid there alone thinking about what I was going to do. I knew that was not my idea of a marriage. How did I get in that mess in the first place?

After about two hours of sleep, I woke up to Gina screaming.

"Why didn't you come and take Rome to school!? He is your child, and that's the least you can do. I can't keep on taking care of him while you out there whoring around, Brea."

I just hung up the phone. Today was not the day. The man I married doesn't love me and is probably having another child by his baby's mom. The last thing I wanted to hear was Gina's high-pitched voice squealing through the phone. I picked myself up and called Draya.

"Draya, can you come over here please? I really need to talk to someone."

She could tell I had been crying, because my voice was raspy as if I had a cold.

Without hesitation, she said, "I'm on my way."

I managed to put on some clothes. I had to go to school and then the shop afterwards, but I was not going to make it because I felt like crap. When Draya got finally made it, she ran up the steps and entered without bothering to knock.

"Brea, what happened? Why you look like that? What did Gene say?"

I told her about dinner and how he really didn't say anything. I also told her how he kicked me down the stairs. I had been through worse, but for some reason I could not stop crying. She was speechless for a second as she tried to find the words to help me feel better.

"We should go to her house. I mean, I'll fuck that bitch up," she said quickly.

I wasn't a fighter, but her words reminded me that I wrote down Kia's number as I was going through the messages. Bingo! I would just call her up and see what she had to say. Although I wanted answers, I was too scared to make the call but Draya wasn't. My hands were shaking and my palms were sweeting so badly. After pushing *67 to block my number, I dialed the number very slowly. It started ringing, and I pushed it off to Draya. When Kia answered, Draya immediately went crazy.

"Listen, bitch. This is Brea, Gene's wife. We are married, and you need to stop fucking with him and leave us alone."

All I could hear was laughter through the phone.

"Wife? Bitch please, everyone knows I'm the wife. I know who the fuck you are. He just left here. What you wanna know since you big and bad?" Kia responded nonchalantly.

She began to say how she was pregnant and he took her to the abortion clinic that morning. She said she had been with him for eight years, and he was never going to leave her. She knew about me but thought I was just the new fling for him. Draya got quiet and handed me the phone. She was whispering to me while she had the receiver of the phone covered with her hand.

"Tell her everything, Brea. You need to do this, not me." I grabbed the phone and hoped she didn't notice the voice change.

"Did he tell you we got legally married a few months ago?" I asked.

"Fuck no. Ain't no way he married someone else."

After exchanging stories about Gene, we decided to meet at a park. I was scary and didn't like confrontation, so I wanted to meet somewhere in the open. Draya agreed to drive me but sit in the car.

"I'll be in the car if you need me. I will fuck that bitch up. Just say the word," Draya said as she stared at Kia.

"It's cool, Draya. I just want the truth."

Draya was always on go, and she was known to whoop quite a few bitches' asses. I walked up to Kia wearing my red leather jacket and red leather Enzo boots that I got from Gene as a gift. The funny thing is, we looked just alike. We were both brown-skinned and thin with long hair. It was weird. We even talked alike.

She showed me all the messages in her phone about him telling her how much he loved her and wanted them to work. I showed her the marriage certificate. She took a deep breath and swallowed really hard. Damn, she was just as hurt as I was, if not more. To think she had been with him all those years, and I only knew him a few months yet I had the last name. I actually felt some form of gratification knowing that.

When Kia finally gathered her words, she replied, "I'm done. You can have his ass. That's your husband, and I'm not looking stupid no more for this nigga. I don't care how many kids we got."

I didn't say anything else. I just walked off and hopped in the Benz with Draya.

"Draya, what am I going to do? I mean, I don't know what to do. I am not going back to Gina's house."

"You know you can come stay with me, girl."

To be honest, I really didn't want to stay with her either. I just wanted my very own happy life. She dropped me off at home. By then, I had five messages from Gina. I decided to call her back. As usual, she was just yelling in the phone.

I finally screamed, "Gene and I are married, and I found out that he's been cheating! His baby's mom just had an abortion today! Please cut me some slack today! PLEASE."

She just laughed at me and replied, "Why would you marry someone you don't even know? You so fuckin stupid, Brea."

I could hear her pause to sip that darn extra black coffee she liked. She really got satisfaction out of my pain.

"Just leave Rome here tonight. Wait until Mark hears how stupid your ass is."

Mark? Really? Why did he even need to know anything? I just said okay and hung up the phone. I had a feeling Gene knew what had happened. I'm sure Kia told him. I waited up for him to come home.

I began daydreaming and wondering what life would be like if he loved me. Maybe like Cliff Huxtable loved Claire and Dwayne loved Whitley?

I made his favorite meatloaf and waited patiently. The red sauce aroma lingered throughout the house as I fell asleep on the sofa. Finally, he came in and woke me up. He told me the whole story and kept apologized. He promised that he loved me, and he was going to be faithful to me and only me. He even said that he told her to never call him unless it was about the kids. I didn't believe him even though I wanted to. Tears streamed down my face while he professed his love for me. He wiped all my tears and began to kiss me and suck on my titties, as if that would make me feel better. It didn't. I didn't need sex. I needed love - real love. I blacked out during sex and pretty much just laid there. I was so over the whole situation. I was so over my life. I really started to hate living and became very depressed.

Nothing really changed much after I found out he cheated on me. We stayed together, and I just tried to live a normal life. That is...until one day I decided that I wanted revenge - I mean *real* revenge. Mike was the man in the game, no doubt. I mean, Gene was no slouch, and he was definitely affording us a decent lifestyle. I enjoyed the finer things in life. You know a Navigator truck, banging house, and the fancy restaurants. But, I swear I would have settled just to be loved. I knew he was still messing with his baby's mom. That lying bitch couldn't get enough of my husband. He did come home most nights, but he mostly stayed out just like before I found out. We didn't really have a relationship. We were more like roommates. I was leaving for school and work when he was coming in from God knows where. His kids would come over on the weekends, and I would get Rome more. Gina was losing her mind, so he was spending more and more time with me. I barely went over there to see them because she was always drunk, and I just didn't want or need the drama. By this time, things were about to take a turn for the worse. My 21st birthday was coming up and unbeknownst to me, Draya and Gene were planning a big party for me at the local bar. I really didn't care that it was my birthday, since I was somewhat over life. I actually hated life at this point and used to pray that I would just die.

Draya convinced me to come over to her house on my birthday. She took me to get my nails done, and we went shopping at our favorite mall at that time, King of Prussia. I loved Armani Exchange, and I think Draya meant well, but shopping couldn't fix me.

"Girl, I'm taking you out and getting you drunk - pissy drunk, so cheer up! Brea, he said sorry, and he's been doing right. Let a man be a man."

I hated that fucking saying *let a man be a man*. Believe it or not, after we left, I was actually feeling better for the first time in a while. I had on a bangin' Versace dress and the gold emblem stood out with some gold sandals. I loved getting my makeup done by Draya, because she was great at getting jazzed up. I did my own hair, and I was feeling myself. We took my black Navigator that Gene had gotten detailed earlier, so you could smell the new car air freshener as we headed out to for the evening. I was so ready to have a good time.

We pulled up at some bar in Philly that had valet parking. We were feeling and looking like a million bucks, literally. I stepped in first and was amazed to see a bunch of people screaming, *SURPRISE!* I was so shocked that Tia was there along with Rhonda or Ronnie or whatever he was going by, and even Mark and his wife were there. Mostly everyone else were friends of Draya or Gene. I could smell the fried chicken and collard greens coming from the kitchen. The place was packed, and I was very happy for the moment. I was dancing, eating, and enjoying myself. I had so much fun that by the end of the night, I had my shoes off, and I was percolating on the dance floor.

"It's time for the percolator! Go ahead Brea, that's your song!" Draya said as we laughed and continued to dance.

I didn't know what I was doing, but with Draya cheering me on, I had nothing to lose. I must say, it was probably the best night I had my entire life. I felt really loved. Everybody was crazy drunk.

Mike showed up to get Draya when the party was almost over. He walked in with an attitude because he was a control freak, and Draya was a free spirit as well as a huge flirt. He happened to walk in while she was hanging onto some guy and slurring her words. The funny thing is, she would never cheat on him even though he had a wife. Gene told me to drive with him, so I let Rhonda take my car back to Gina's. I would get it the next morning. We lived further down the highway than Draya did, and Gene was so drunk. I was drunk as well, as a result, he

drove to Draya's house and said we were staying
there. When we got there, Mike was outside and
Gene just walked past him. I asked him where Draya
was, and he looked mad and said she was upstairs
throwing up in her bathroom. I ran up to check on
her. Gene was already asleep on the floor. Draya was
half-naked with her face in the toilet. She was
moaning and mumbling, and the smell of her throw
up and flowery perfume almost made me sick.

"Brea, I hate that muthafucka. He ain't never
gonna leave her, and I hate his bitch ass."

I had never heard her talk about Mike like
that. She always talked good about him, but my
daddy always said drunk people and kids tell the
truth. I helped her get in the bed and just left her in
her red panty and bra set. I wrapped her up in her
black satin sheets. Then, I quietly took my shoes off
and opened her top dresser draw and grabbed a
pajama short set for myself. As I closed the door
quietly, I could feel someone behind me. When I
turned around, it was Mike.

"Where you going? You can sleep in the other
room," he said with a weird look in his eyes.

"That's cool. I'll just sleep on the sofa."

"I don't want you fucking up my sofa. That
shit is expensive."

I didn't want to hear his mouth, so I just
walked to the other room that their son slept in since
he wasn't home. Mike followed me and stood in the
doorway.

"Did you have a good birthday, because you
surely looked good?"

Was he coming on to me? He had never said more than two words to me, and now he wanted to have this long drawn out conversation.

"It was straight, but I'm tired, and I really need to go to sleep."

"Cool. Goodnight, Brea."

That was very weird, but I just laid down and went to sleep. Shortly after I dozed off, I woke up to the smell of black and mild and this nigga Mike with his head between my legs. It was too late to even stop him, because I was about to cum. He looked me in the eye, and we started kissing with Draya in one room and Gene in the other. I was about to fuck the man of my cousin who happened to be the only person that really cared about me. Before I knew it, we were fucking, and it was so damn good. What the fuck was I doing? Draya loved him. Even though I felt bad, I didn't check out. I was all in.

He came inside of me, and I didn't even realize that he didn't have on a condom. Damn, why did he do that shit? Realistically, I was raped, but I didn't try to stop him. So was it really rape just because I was drunk? Without saying another word, he jumped up and left the room. Gene was his best friend and my husband. I couldn't go back to sleep, so I laid there for a while and just thought about what I had just done. I felt a little vindicated because I fucked Gene's best friend. On the other hand, I felt bad because Draya had my back. What the fuck did I just do? Regardless of how bad I felt, I was not going to say a word. I decided to just keep my mouth shut like I did about everything else as I tried to bury the sexcapade that I had with my cousin's only love and my husband's best friend.

Chapter 6 - The Setup

After the incident at Draya's house, I was really trying to avoid her by all means because I did not want to face her. She was calling and calling, and Gene kept asking me why I wasn't talking with her. I just brushed it off. I felt bad that I did that to Draya, because I knew she really loved him and me. I was almost finished with hair school and working more hours at the salon. It was summer, so Rome was out of school. He spent most of the summer with Jerome and his family, so I really didn't see him that much. When Rome wasn't at the house, Gene didn't get his kids. I really didn't have a relationship with them, and I really didn't care to have one since I knew he was still fucking their mother. Unfortunately, I couldn't prove it, and I wasn't leaving even if I did, so I just stayed married. One day I would get enough money to open my own shop and move out west with Tia.

Tia loved Cali, and she looked so refreshed and vibrant when she came home for my party. She was a true LA girl. She rushed home right after my party and had no interest in being on the East Coast at all. I was working hard and graduating in August. I was determined to finish school. It was so hot that summer, and I remember riding to work blasting some reggae with the windows down. That's what we used to do. Everyone was hanging outside on every corner, and they had the fire hydrants going. I loved the summer but hated it at the same time. The summer also meant people would be acting stupid and killing each other. I went to seven funerals that year alone for people that Gene knew. I knew of them either through him, or I may have gone to school with some of them. It seemed like the stupidity got worse in the summer time. I would always worry about Gene because he was always in the streets, or so he said.

One Friday after a long day at the shop, I locked up everything and got ready to leave. It wasn't late, but it was dark. As I walked out to the car, I saw Mike standing by my truck. Was he crazy? Why was he here?

"Open the door and let me get in and talk to you real fast."

"Mike, that's not a good idea. I really gotta get home, you know."

He snatched the keys from me, pushed the unlock button, and jumped in the driver's seat. I really didn't want to deal with that shit. I hopped in the passenger seat after moving all of my books and junk that I had on the front seat. He drove to a dark alley and parked. When he rolled down the windows, all I could smell was the piss from the alley.

"Listen, Brea. I'm sorry about what happened between us the night of the party. I was drunk and shouldn't have come on to you. But, I can't lie. You are so damn sexy, and I want you so bad."

Meanwhile, he rubbed his dick while he half-way apologized.

"Ok, Mike, let's just forget about it. You know I love Gene, and you love Draya."

He reached over and kissed me, but I refused. I was punching him and telling him to stop, but he just wouldn't.

"Don't fight me. You know you want it! Just take it."

I really didn't want it, but he overpowered me. He dragged me into the backseat of the Navi and leaned the seat forward. Then, he raped me. It was definitely rape this time, because I was not a willing participant at all. I did not want to have sex with this man again. I just wished that he would leave me alone. As he was inside of me, I reverted back to that little girl and remembered when Gina left me alone. I began to pray silently and suddenly he stopped. I don't know if he came or not, I was just so happy that he'd stopped. He drove me back to the shop in silence. I know he could see how upset I was, but he didn't care.

"What you crying for? You should be happy a nigga like me wanna fuck your ass. You know how many bitches throw the pussy at me. You got the game fucked up, baby girl."

As he exited my truck to get into his car, I slid over to the driver's seat, and he licked my face with his long, pink tongue. He hopped in his Buick and sped off very fast. He never drove a nice car, because he didn't want the attention.

I sat there for about thirty minutes crying my eyes out. I just wanted to be done with that Mike shit. Why was I always the damn victim? I needed to tell Draya. I really needed her to know what this man was doing. I didn't do anything wrong. He was pretty much forcing me. She would be hurt, but she would believe me. I had to figure out a way to tell her. Now Gene was another issue. I think he loved Mike more than Draya did. They had been friends for years, and Gene would take a bullet for him. As a matter of fact, he did when they were younger. Back in high school, someone was coming for Mike and Gene jumped in front of the bullet that was meant for Mike. It only grazed him, but he was willing to die for that man. I didn't know how I was going to tell him, and I was having second thoughts about the whole thing. I finally got up the nerve to talk to Draya, although I hadn't spoken with her in weeks. I went to her house, and she hugged me.

"Girl, why you ain't been answering my phone calls? What the hell is wrong with you?"

"I've just been busy with school, work, and trying to make my marriage work, you know."

Only if she knew that I was avoiding her because her nasty boyfriend kept coming on to me. I felt so bad.

"Girl, I know you hurt about that Gene shit. I know you ain't got a good man like me, but Gene is cool. He's decent, so just hang in there."

I mumbled under my breath, "Good man? Yeah right," but she didn't hear that.

I was really quiet and trying to work up the nerve to tell her, but I couldn't. What if she didn't believe me and tried to fight me? She was known to fight anybody over Mike, even though he was married. She even cut his wife and was on probation for the shit. I wasn't a fighter, so I wasn't taking any chances. I made up a story about having to go get Rome. I hadn't seen my son in days, but I didn't want to deal with Gina. Daddy had been calling me, and I just avoided him, too. I knew Gina had told him about Gene cheating on me and that we were married, so I didn't want to even hear my daddy at the time.

I drove around for hours trying to figure out what I could possibly do. Telling Gene and Draya was out of the question, because it would back fire on me. I just had a feeling that it wouldn't work in my favor, so I just didn't say anything. When I got home, Gene wasn't there, and that pissed me off even more. Every night when I got home, he was out in the streets or more than likely with Kia. I felt so low at that very moment, yet I had no one to turn to for comfort. I remember talking to myself in the bathroom and wishing I had that $150K that P had stashed. I would have been out of that hell hole then. Unfortunately, I didn't have the money, and I was living my reality. While I sulked about my horrible life, I drunk a pint of Seagram's Gin. I cried and talked to myself as I realized that I was looking and sounding a lot like Gina. By the time I got to the bottom of the bottle, I was ready for war. Hell, I was really tired of being the victim. I was going to call Draya and tell her. I ran into the kitchen to grab the cordless phone off the charger. I remember dialing the number, and at about the third ring, a man answered.

"Hello, who this?"

Damn, it was Mike. I didn't say anything. I just hung up. *Damnit!!* I thought as I started hitting the wall. All I can recall was being in the bathroom crying and foaming at the mouth when my hand started bleeding. Somehow I'd made my way to the glass mirror when I was abusing the wall, which explained how I had a big, bloody gash on my hand. We had these plush tan rugs that couldn't disguise the blood no matter what. There were red blood drops all over the floor. *Why the fuck did I do that?* I washed my hand which was swelling up due to pieces of broken glass underneath my skin. Loose pieces of glass dropped down the drain along with the bloody water. The phone was ringing, but I didn't get it. I wrapped a towel around my hand and dozed off from the alcohol that seeped through my pores. The next thing I remember was waking up to Gene shaking me.

"Brea, what the fuck happened?"

"I cut my hand. I'm sorry," I replied.

I was drunk and felt dizzy. He forced me to go to the ER. We sat in that ice cold waiting area with those bright lights for what seemed like hours. Finally, after Gene cussed the staff out, I was taken to the back. Gene kept asking me what happened and why I had done that, but I didn't say anything. I just wanted to go to sleep. After being in the hospital for hours, they gave me some Percocet for the pain, and they applied a brace on my fractured hand. I would not be able to use my right hand for about six weeks.

Gene must have called Gina the next morning, because she was at my house with Rome that afternoon. As a mother, you would think she came to make sure I was okay. Of course she came to critique the house instead while she called me stupid and asked what I was thinking. I was so sick of living. I took two pills while she was there, and after about ten minutes, whatever she was saying didn't matter. She kept telling Gene to watch me because I'd had issues since I was a child. Shit, who wouldn't have issues after the shit I endured? Rome wanted to stay with me, which was odd, but I was cool with that. Gina and Gene both left, and I was home alone with

Rome. For the first time, we really sat and talked. He was only six years old, but he was so smart. Looking at him made me want to be a better mom. I wanted to be more for him and have more in life. We laid in bed all night watching the *Land Before Time* movies. It was so cool.

I remember him looking up to me saying, "Mom, I love you. Let's do this again," and then he went to sleep in my arms.

At about 4 a.m., the house phone rung, and I answered it in my sleepy voice, "Hello?"

"Um yeah, Gene is over here. Can you come get your man? I keep telling him to go home to his wife."

It was his fuckin baby's mom after that nigga swore on his kids that he wasn't seeing her. All lies.

"No, bitch, you can have him. Tell him he's not welcome here."

I was done. I wasn't going to take it anymore. I hung up the phone and looked around the house. It was so peaceful just my son and I. That's how it should have been. I needed to be worried about my son, not Mike, Gene or Draya. I had to get them out of my life. How it was going to happen, I didn't know yet. Gene came home the next day as usual. This time, he smelled like sex and had on the same clothes from the day before. He didn't even have enough decency to wash his ass. He usually smelled like dove soap when he came in, but he was getting more and more disrespectful. I left without saying goodbye and dropped Rome off at Gina's. I had one hand in a brace but I was still able to drive even though I wasn't supposed to put the strain on my arm. I pulled out the pain pills that were prescribed to me. Although the directions said to take one every 4-6 hours, I decided to take two. The feeling I got was amazing, and I didn't have a care in the world.

I drove to Draya's house without calling. I usually called ahead of time out of respect but, I did not this time. I didn't knock since I still had a key. I entered I ran upstairs prepared to tell my cousin about her triflin ass nigga.

"Draya, where are you? I have to tell you something right now."

She came running out the back looking confused.

"What the fuck is wrong with you, girl?"

She sat down on the sofa but not before grabbing her bottle of Asti Spumante champagne from the kitchen. I started tearing up as I told her that Mike had hit on me, but I didn't tell her about the sexcapade that we had or the episode in the car when he raped me. I just said he tried to kiss me. She started laughing hysterically.

"No offense, Brea, but why would Mike want you? He don't even like you. As a matter of fact, he can't stand you and you too dark for him. He don't like chocolate girls, and he probably was drunk."

I just dropped my head, then I looked in her eyes and could see that she really did not believe me. She gave me a drink and told me to hold on as she got up from her seat. She went to the back room and returned with Mike walking behind her.

"Brea, tell Mike what you said he did, since you ain't lying."

Why was my favorite cousin doing this to me? She was supposed to be my ride or die. At least that's what she led me to believe.

"Mike, please tell her what happened."

Mike looked at me and said nothing. I guess he was trying to gather his thoughts, because he finally said something, BUT it wasn't what I expected. He admitted to having sex with me, but he told her that I kept coming on to him, and he was drunk so he gave in to me. In a split second, Draya jumped over the table and started punching me in the face and in my stomach. She was even kicking me and she kept bending my injured arm back. She was so furious. I finally broke loose and ran down the steps. My hurt quickly turned into anger as I hopped in the truck and began to talk to myself. I didn't even want to go home. Blood was leaking from my eye. At the time, I thought it was sweat until I saw the blood on my hand after wiping my eye. My hand was throbbing, and I knew I couldn't drive. I made a rash decision to go to Gina's since her house was the closest. I ran into the house and Gina was downstairs. Daddy was in the basement watching TV, and Rome was upstairs playing video games. I crept quietly into the house. "Hey, Gina. Can I stay here tonight? I was in a fight with Draya, and I don't want to go home."

Unsurprisingly, she shot me down instantly and made it clear that I was grown and married and that she couldn't be involved with my affairs. She kept telling me that I needed to grow up, and I didn't even say anything. I just left out of the house and sat behind the wheel of my truck. My mind was racing, and I was in pain. The only person I had left to tell was my husband, the man who was cheating on me with his ex. Sadly, he never stopped messing with her during the time we had been married. Hell, it wasn't a real marriage. It was all a lie.

I finally decided to go home after being gone all day. To my surprise, Gene was there when I got home. It was as if he was waiting for me, because something felt odd. I walked in the house, and he didn't even look at me when he spoke.

"You fucked my boy, Brea. That's my brother. How could you do some shit like that?"

"I didn't. He raped me, and he kept coming on to me. I begged him to stop."

He was pacing around the floor and punching his fist into the opposite hand.

"Gene, you believe me right? I swear I wouldn't do that to you."

Tears began to come from his eyes and in that second, I knew something in him believed me.

His voice cracked a bit as he said, "I should have took that nigga out the last time he did this shit."

He proceeded to tell me about a time when he caught Mike fucking his first girlfriend and how she had told Gene that he forced her. He said that he didn't want to believe that since they had been more like brothers than friends for so many years. I reached out to hug him from the side, but he pushed me away.

"Brea, your mom told me you lie a lot and that you shot your dad when you were a kid. With that being said, I'm having a hard time believing this shit."

Why did people always flip flop on me? He knew I was telling the truth, but he was still acting as if he didn't believe me. I was getting tired of people using me and then throwing me away like I didn't matter. I was tired of crying because no one really cared about me at all. Now, he was taking what Gina told him, but only if he really knew that she was the crazy one. He looked at me, grabbed a bag, and started shoving stuff into it.

"I'm out. I'm done with you. I can't be married to a fucking slut. I should have known you wasn't shit. I gotta believe my brother. You ain't even Mike type. You got thirty days to get the fuck out, and don't ever call me again."

As he walked down the stairs, I don't know what emotion came over me, but I was furious. I wanted to kill him, Draya, and Mike. I wished I was strong enough to kill them all. How could they do this to me? I opened the glass sliding door that led to the patio. I grabbed the bottle of gin and the pills that I had before going out and started to plot. The Gina in me was coming out. I wasn't going to let these muthafuckers get away with this. There was no fucking way. I had a plan. They all were in the drug game, and Draya did a lot of drug transactions for Mike. Her house was the damn stash house. I knew that, because Draya would talk a lot and tell me all the business when she got drunk. I was going to call the cops, but I had to be smart. I wanted all of them to suffer. I had thirty days to come up with a plan, a good plan. I wasn't working at this time, and I only had about $3,000 saved, but that would still give me a chance to move on my own.

In those next thirty days, I would beg Draya to talk to me, so I could throw her off my plan. She would never believe it was me, because she thought I was stupid. I may have been a little late to respond,

but I was never stupid. I made sure I also called
Gene and left multiple messages. Neither of them
called me back, but my phone calls were "proof" that
I wanted to make peace with them. I was home for
the next few weeks planning and plotting. I looked at
a two-bedroom apartment, and I was going to pay the
rent up for a few months with the money I had
stashed. I planned to get Rome and change my life
because I was going to live right. I was going to be a
mom, and maybe a wife to a real husband who loved
me for me. At that time, all I wanted was to be loved.
I had my plan all mapped out.

Every Friday night, they would get drunk at
Draya's house. It was the thing they did, and they
never changed their routine. I would set them up on
that day. I knew the house would be packed, and I
knew all of them would be there. On top of that, I
knew they wouldn't suspect me, because a lot of
people disliked Mike, but they tolerated him. With all
the heartfelt messages I left Draya and Gene, they
wouldn't even begin to think it was me. I decided to
get a smoker to make the call to the cops for me, but
I needed it to be a smoker that wasn't from the city
since everyone knew them. I went to one of the grimy
areas in Philly where all the homeless people were
and gave a bum $40 to make the call. There was a
drug task force unit that accepted anonymous tips
from callers. I had the bum to report their drug
activity and where they would gather every Friday.
After giving clear instructions and making the
payment, I got back into my truck feeling
accomplished. They would all pay for what they had
put me through.

When Friday came, I was excited like it was my birthday. I hadn't heard from Gene or Draya at all. They didn't even try to call just to hear me out. They actually believed I had done something wrong. I even left messages for Gene telling him it was important, yet I he didn't give me a call back or anything. I drove past Draya's house and saw everyone's cars parked out front, so I knew they were all there. After that, I went to Gina's since I hadn't seen Rome in weeks. I had love for my son, but I really didn't know how to be his mom. Gina was his mom. As usual, Gina was cold when I entered the house. I went straight to the basement with daddy and watched Jeopardy as we often did in silence. This once vibrant, amazing man was slipping away to nothing. I wish my poor dad had a backbone and left Gina, because she was no good for him.

As I sat watching TV with my dad, I wondered had the drug task force gotten them yet. It was still early, and I didn't know what time or even if they were coming. All I knew was that they were going to get them, and I was happy. I fell asleep watching TV and it was very late by the time I woke up. I headed out past Gina who slumped on the sofa with a bottle of vodka in one hand and empty pill bottles on the floor. Her house robe was halfway open and exposing her saggy titties. I stepped over all of that trash and headed out the door. It was so dark, and all I could hear was the typical sirens and music playing from the passing cars. I headed down the highway to my house. I was tempted to ride past Draya's to see if they had been raided yet, but I decided to just go home. When I got there, someone grabbed me from behind and scared the shit out of me.

"Brea, they got Mike and Draya! They're coming for me, and I know it," Gene said in a low, frantic voice.

What the fuck was Gene doing there, and why was he not locked up? I acted like I didn't know what was going on, as he explained what happened. He said that they were all chillin' at the house like normal, and he had left to go to the liquor store. He would usually go to the one right by the house, but he went to one across town instead. When he got back, he saw the task force bringing out Draya, Mike, and the six other people that were in the house. I really wanted him gone too, but seeing him there made me want to be there for him. He could have gone to Kia's house, but he came to me. I was his wife. It could be us against the world now that Mike and Draya were gone. Even though I had set that shit up, I could just be supportive. As a matter of fact, I did need his money, because $3000 wasn't going to take me far. Plus, I had already started dipping into it. With those two out of the picture, maybe we could be the happy family that I always dreamed of being. He could work on his music and not have to sell dope, and I could just focus on getting my salon open and getting Rome with me.

I could see that he was scared, so I used that to my advantage. When we went to bed, I told him everything that happened the night of my 21st birthday party. He just listened and didn't say much about it. After that, I kept telling him how he could be the man with Mike gone, but he had to be smart. He had to go hard with the music and the drug game, and eventually put that drug shit to bed. Then, we could get out of Jersey and maybe hit Cali with Tia or the ATL with my transgender brother Rhonda. He was sold on my ideas, and for the first time in our relationship, I think this nigga was actually listening to me. I had turned the tables, and the ball was in my court. I had flipped the script on this nigga, and I was winning.

Come to find out, they had found a lot of drugs and money in Draya's house. They took her child from her, and she and Mike didn't even have a bail, so they were not getting out anytime soon. Gene and I would be long gone by the time they even got a court date. Mike started calling Gene through a third party, and Gene would put money on his books. He couldn't risk talking to him directly, so he wouldn't be implicated in the indictment as well. Unbeknownst to me, Mike was wanted on some murder shit, so that nigga wasn't never getting out. It was all in the newspaper, and they were trying to railroad Mike as the leader and Draya as his right-hand woman. This was true to a certain extent. Mike's wife was not a part of it at all, and she made sure her hands were clean. She was a RN or some shit. Gene and I were really trying to make it work, and he was even staying home every night. I still didn't trust that nigga, and I knew things would never be right since they were crazy from the start, but I stayed and tried to be a family. I never told him about the setup, because I know he would have killed me. I just lived life day to day hoping to get the hell away from my life one day soon.

Chapter 7 - So you're Having My Baby?

After a few months, the hype behind me setting Draya and Mike up had died down. Gene was still handling the drug business and laundering money into his music studio and into the barbershop he had set up. He made sure Mike was straight. We didn't hear much of Draya, but word on the street was that she was not doing well in jail. Her mom had custody of her son. I only got this little bit of information from the go-to person that Gene had relaying information to Mike. I finally had my cosmetology license, and I was doing hair at the house. I was the best kitchen beautician there was, and everyone wanted me to do their hair. I really wanted my own shop, but Gene would always say we had to be smart with money, so I just patiently waited. He was a smart guy, and we started to get closer than ever. His baby's mom was even respecting our marriage, and she had a boyfriend. I could finally have my husband to myself, or so I thought.

Rome and Gene's kids would come over every weekend, and we did a lot of family stuff together. We were really turning into the Brady bunch, and I was cool with that. However, the kids did get on my nerves, and I started becoming more dependent on pills and alcohol just like Gina had. Gene would get pills from some white boy that he was dealing with, and he was cool with me taking them since they made me very mellow and more sexual. Of course he loved that because the real Brea was not sexual at all. Most of the time, I was high or drunk when I had sex which made the experience easier to handle. We went from having sex once a week to getting it in about two times a day. It was very enjoyable, especially when I was on Percocet or Vicodin. If Gene couldn't get me any, I would fake tooth pain and get my own prescription.

After a year of constant sex with my husband, I discovered I was pregnant, and he was so happy. We had talked about having a little girl one day, so you can say it was planned. We sat the kids down one weekend and told them. Rome was not happy, and he still didn't like me because Gina had him brainwashed. Gene's kids were very happy. I didn't get the chance to tell Gina because the mouth of the south Rome beat me to it. This kid was seven years old going on seventy-seven. He would tell Gina everything. One weekend when the kids were over, Rome heard us having sex. He told Gina when he got home, and she called me in an uproar.

"Brea, y'all shouldn't have sex when Rome is there. That's disgusting, and you all need to do that when he is not there."

I couldn't believe she had called me about having sex with my own husband in my own house. Who does that? The same woman that let some man molest her kids was trying to tell me what to do with mine. Rome got on my fucking nerves. I couldn't stand his ass, but I know now that I was very jealous of him. After he told Gina about me being pregnant when I told him not to, caused me to abuse him more. I didn't physically abuse him, but the mental abuse was brutal. When he would come over, I would threaten to kill him if he told Gina anything. He was a fat little boy, and I would take snacks from him and give him all vegetables as punishment for telling

Gina stuff. He would have to eat vegetables while all the other kids were able to have snacks. I couldn't wait until Monday to get him back to his favorite person - his grandma.

Overall, things were pretty much as normal as could be for a girl like me. I was pregnant by my husband, and we were happy. I wasn't a teenager anymore, so things were different. No one looked at me like I had two heads, and people actually congratulated me. It was a whole new experience. I didn't feel ashamed or embarrassed. It was weird, but I was rolling with the punches. Gene and I had been dating and even going to a local church as a family. I was loving the idea of the family life that I always wanted. About ten weeks into my pregnancy, Gene started acting weird. He was staying out late again causing my brain to wonder if he was back messing with Kia. One of his sons did mention that her live-in boyfriend had moved out, but I was cautious not to press the issue. He was still being a great husband as far as I could tell. He gave me whatever I wanted, and I was so happy to have a man to love me and treat me good. He was making a lot more money, so I just thought maybe he was handling business.

Even though I had my suspicions about Gene, I continued life as usual until some information fell in my lap one day while I was doing this lady's hair. Her name was Ms. Bessy, but I used to call her Messy Bessy, because all she did was talk about people. I had only done her hair a few times before. She was like the old lady on *In Living Color* that would say, "I ain't the one to gossip, so you ain't heard that from me." That was Ms. Bessy. She wasn't very old, but I called her Ms. because she was old enough to be my mother. She knew all the local gossip and then some. She was going on and on about the lady up the street from her whose kids got taken away and the other lady whose husband was sleeping with her brother. I really didn't care to hear any of it, but I just listened and tried to finish her hair as quickly as I could.

As we were talking, I felt a little lightheaded and nauseous with me being pregnant and all, so I stopped to eat and take a break. She was annoyed that I was stopping, so I decided to tell her that I was pregnant. I was not showing, so I really didn't have to tell her. She looked at me up and down and started laughing. I didn't know what she was laughing at, so I just smiled and keep on eating.

"So you okay with Lakeethea being pregnant the same time as you? You a good woman, Brea," she laughed.

I didn't know who the hell she was talking about, so I stopped eating and looked at her like she was crazy.

"Who is Lakeethea?"

She quickly blurted, "Your husband has three kids by her and a fourth on the way, and you don't know her name?"

I swallowed fast when I remembered that Kia's full name was Lakeethea. I never called her that, so it didn't hit me until she said my husband had kids by her. Immediately, I became so confused.

"Ms. Bessy, if she is pregnant, which I doubt, it's not by Gene. You are clearly mistaken."

She sucked her teeth so hard as she rolled her eyes and began to tell me that she knew that Kia was pregnant. She said that she was showing and looked to be about six or seven months. Even if that was true, I just knew she wasn't pregnant by Gene. *There is no way*, I thought as I got up and finished doing Messy Bessy's hair.

"I'm sorry, honey. I wasn't tryna be messy. I just don't know how you can stay married to a man that has all those children by the same woman. He must love her to keep having babies by her," she said trying to sound concerned.

"Ms. Bessy, no offense, but I know you are mistaken. She has a man, so she's probably pregnant by him not my husband."

She just rolled her eyes, took the $50 out of her breast, waited for her $5 change and left. That old huzzy crumbled my world with her words and still left without tipping. I couldn't wait to call Gene. He answered right away. I didn't mention what I had just heard, since I had to investigate for myself. Ms. Bessy always got the story wrong, but my daddy would always say that behind every rumor, there is some truth. I was sure about to get down to the bottom of it. I was too invested in my relationship, and this would not mess my family up. I played it cool when Gene came home. I cooked his favorite meal and even fixed his plate. He loved turkey meatloaf, so I made sure it was ready for him.

After we ate, he pulled me close, sat me on his lap, and said he was ready to move. He wanted to go to Atlanta instead of Cali. My heart was racing, because I had been wanting to get out of Jersey for what seemed like my entire life. I just wanted a fresh start. One problem was that I couldn't help but to wonder if he really had Kia pregnant again. Was Ms.

Bessy right, or was she living up to her name and just being Messy Bessy? I was too scared to say anything.

"Brea, we got enough money to just roll. Mike is set for life, and I want out of this life. I can't end up in jail or dead. It ain't worth it."

I just nodded my head in agreement but remained quiet.

"What's wrong you ok?" he asked.

I just blamed it on being pregnant and told him my hormones were all over the place. He went in the bathroom where we had a Jacuzzi tub and told me to take my clothes off and get in. I really didn't want to have sex. Plus, I remember when I was pregnant with Rome, Gina told me not to take a bath, only a shower, so I was hesitant. Gina was always saying some bullshit, so I didn't really believe her, but it still was in the back of my mind. I decided to get in and he joined me. He was rubbing my back, holding me, and telling me how much he loved me. He began to rub my stomach saying he hoped it was a little girl. He seemed so happy, but I wasn't all that happy. I couldn't help but think about what I was told earlier. I was daydreaming the whole time.

I finally broke my silence and said, "I don't feel well. I'm going to go lay down."

He swooped me up in his arms and carried me to the bed. He kissed me all over and rubbed me down but never attempted to have sex with me. He just laid there and held me. It felt so good and made me remember why I loved him so much. We both fell asleep, but I didn't sleep long. He was lying next to me naked as I eased out of the bed and rushed in the bathroom to grab his pants to retrieve his phone. My heart dropped when I opened the phone. There was message after message from Kia again. This bitch just wouldn't go away! He got his number changed when we decided to make it work, so she was not supposed to have his number. She was only supposed to call the house phone, but that was not happening at all.

They had so many messages that I couldn't even read them all. I was shaking, but I couldn't cry for some reason. I wanted to know if the bitch was pregnant. If she was, I was going to kick the baby out of her fucking stomach. I was not playing this time. I wasn't the best fighter, but I was sick of this bitch. I just wanted her to leave my husband alone and get a damn man. He didn't marry her, he married me. So, why was she so pressed to be with him? I scrolled through all the messages, but none of them proved what Messy Bessy had told me earlier. I quickly put the phone back in his pocket and jumped back in bed. He didn't even budge.

The next morning, he woke me up to breakfast in bed and gave me a long kiss before he left. Once he was gone, I got dressed. I tied my long, black silky hair into a ponytail. It was so wavy and pretty that I had to wet it just to get it to stay. I threw on some sneakers and made sure I wasn't wearing any jewelry, not even my wedding ring. I was going to kill her if she was pregnant by Gene. I'd had enough. I pulled up to Kia's street but parked all the way around the corner. By this time, I knew which apartment she lived in, but I didn't know the exact address. I saw someone standing outside and asked which place was hers, and they quickly gave me the apartment number. Even though I was angry, I didn't know if it was true, so I was most definitely going to hear her out.

I knocked on the door and saw someone peeking out the cheap ass apartment blinds. I could hear the chain lock being taken off and two to three deadbolts being unlocked. She did live in the hood, so I understood the need for extra security. She opened the door and actually invited me in, and this bitch was for sure pregnant. She was a skinny girl like me, so her stomach was easy to notice. She offered me a seat on the cheap fake leather sofa. I sat down on the edge of my seat, because her house was so nasty. I was scared to take any type of roach home. We were all hood, but she was a project chick, and she was proud. She was the type of person that no matter how much money she had or designer clothes she wore, she would always be a project chick. I just straight up asked her was she pregnant. She had somewhat of an attitude when replied to my question.

"Yes, as you can see. I'm clearly pregnant, but why are you over here asking me? Why you ain't ask your husband?"

I could feel the rage in me build up.

"So you're saying you're pregnant by Gene?" I asked her.

"Bitch, are you fucking stupid? Clearly, Gene and I never stopped fucking with your retarded ass, and yes I'm fucking pregnant by him. Gene ain't going nowhere. He chased my man away, girl. We family."

Everything else she said was a blur. I remember standing up and getting ready to go to the door when I saw a small flower pot on her cheap ass end table. I picked up the flower pot, slung it at her, and it hit her straight in the face. Then, I attacked. I was kicking, punching, and biting her. All I remember was kicking her in her pussy on purpose. I wanted her pussy to fall off.

"You stupid bitch! He's my fucking husband! How are you pregnant by somebody's husband and okay with it?!"

She was fighting back, but I got the best of her. For the first time in my life, I was whooping somebody's ass, and it felt good. I wanted to kill her, then I instantly stopped and remembered that I was pregnant. I didn't give a fuck that she was pregnant. Hell, that's why I was kicking her ass.

I ran out the house and headed back down the highway. I had some scratches and my wrist was hurting. I constantly had trouble with it after my fight with the mirror. I hadn't taken any pills or had drank since I found out I was pregnant. I rummaged through the glove box and found a bottle of pills. I took two. I didn't know what it was, but I knew it would have me feeling better soon. After that shit I had just heard, I wasn't about to have no god damn baby no way. I kept calling Gene, but he never answer. When I pulled up at home, I saw his car. I ran in the house and started beating him up, too. He held me down on the floor trying to calm me down, but it wasn't working. I was kicking, punching, and spitting.

"You got that bitch pregnant, Gene! I'm your wife! I thought you loved me! Why why?!"

He just held me down, and I started having flashbacks of when Tim had me held down in the basement. I got the strength to get up in case he tried to rape me just as Tim and Mike had done.

"Fuck you, Gene. You ain't shit," I said as I tried to get up off the floor.

He smacked the piss out of me and started shaking me and telling me to calm down before I lost the baby.

"Fuck this baby, and fuck you!"

I picked up the open bottle of hot sauce and dashed it in his face. Then, I threw the bottle at him. The hot sauce was burning his eyes as he tried to reach for a towel.

"Brea, give me a towel! I can't see!"

I just stood there watching him suffer, I really didn't give a fuck that he was hurt. He had hurt me for the last time. I was done with him, and I was done with life. I was getting the fuck away from him and Jersey. I ran to the car and called Tia. I hadn't talked to her in a while, but we usually talked for hours when we did talk. I told her about the pregnancy, and in true Tia fashion, she told me how dumb I was for getting married. She said I should have been using those niggas because they were using me. She also said that she did not have any room for me, so I could come to Cali but not stay with her. Some friend she was. I had no one. I was parked on a side street while talking to her, so Gene wouldn't come out and find me. He kept calling my phone, and I didn't know what I was going to do. I was feeling high as hell and very nauseous. I somehow made it to Gina's house and pulled her upstairs.

"Listen, I don't need you to be a bitch right now. I need you to be my mom."

The funny thing is, I think she actually smiled when I talked to her that way. I began to tell her what had happened with Kia. I think I just needed someone to talk to for the moment. Like Tia, she made it clear that I could not stay there. She said that she would only take Rome, and neither the new baby nor I could stay. Why I even thought for one second that she would be a real mom to me is beyond me. She kept telling me to work my marriage out and that all men wasn't shit, so I needed to just get over it. Why did everyone think like that? No one believed in love. I was back in my old room looking around and thinking of my next move. I knew I was headed to the abortion clinic for sure. I didn't care if I was married, because I was not going to stay married. This was not the life I wanted.

The next morning I woke up bright and early to make it to the abortion clinic. They had an appointment the next morning, and I was determined to get there. I had some money saved up, but I did not want to go home at all. Gene had been calling Gina's house and leaving me all kinds of messages. He was mostly saying sorry and that he loved me. It was bullshit, and I wasn't falling for it. I was going to kill our child, and I wanted nothing more to do with him. He didn't really love me. No one did. I left out before Gina was up, but I walked right into my dad. I always saw pain in his eyes, and I wanted so desperately to talk to him or just have him hug me and tell me it was going to be okay. However, this was not the Cosby family, and that wasn't going to happen. I just said hi and bye and ran out the door. I was so tired of running in and out of things and life. I just wanted to be normal, whatever that meant.

When I got to the house, Gene wasn't there and I was so relieved. I went into the walk-in closet and got one of my purses that I had stashed in the back of the closet. I grabbed all of the money that I had saved. It was about $3500. I knew the abortion was about $500, and I needed to stay somewhere besides with Gina. I packed a bag good enough for a weekend and hit the door. Before leaving, I left Gene a note with a bunch of FUCK YOUs on it. Looking back, I guess I could have said something more profound, but that's all I could think of at the time. I went to a local motel and just sat and reflected on my life. I didn't sleep much. I remembered that I was not to eat after midnight since I was being put to sleep, so I ate a whole bunch before then.

I cried so much that it looked like I had been in a fight because my eyes were puffy and damn near closed the next morning. I called the local cab company to take me, and I always asked for a lady to pick me up because someone had to walk me in and sign for me. When she got there, I made sure to tell her the deal and pay her extra so she would come in with me and walk me out. This bitch was hip to the game. She wanted an extra $100 to do that. I just gave it to her, because I wanted to get it over with quickly. We pulled up to the same place that I had frequented many times before. I wasn't even sad this time. I was hungry and eating those graham crackers they gave me after surgery was like eating a filet mignon. I went back, paid the money, and waited forever. That place was always packed.

One of the nurses actually remembered me, but I didn't say anything. I laid back on the cold table, and the nurse told me to look up at the big white light, and in 5, 4, 3, 2, 1 I was asleep. I remember waking up in that cold recovery room with a pad between my legs. I did get my graham crackers, and I was back out the door into the same cab headed to the motel. I slept the pain and the rest of the day away. I had about fifty messages from Gene, Gina, and even Rome. I'm sure Gina put him up to calling me, but I didn't even respond. I didn't want to talk to anyone. I just wanted to plot my next move, and I wanted it to be my best move. I needed a fresh start, and the way my life was going, anywhere would be better than where I was at the moment.

Chapter 8 - Welcome to Hotlanta

After staying at the motel for about four days and not talking to anyone, I knew it was time to go home - well to Gina's. I figured she would get the police involved pretty soon and act like she cared that I was missing. I had not showered or changed clothes in all of those days, so I just wanted to go home and wash up. I pulled up to Gina's and Gene's car was the first thing I saw. I wanted to pull off, but I was going to face it all and move on with my life. I walked in and Rome hugged me, but I didn't hug him back. I didn't know how to love him. Gina rolled her eyes and took Rome upstairs.

Daddy just hugged me and said, "I'm glad you're okay baby girl," before he disappeared down the basement stairs.

I was left alone in the living room with Gene. He immediately started pleading his case again.

"Brea, I was so worried. I love you, girl. Real talk. I only want you. My BM not pregnant by me."

No matter what he said, I knew it was all a lie. I sat down and listened to him going on and on about how he wanted to make his family work. He kept asking how I was feeling and about the baby, but I didn't respond. Finally, I told him I was in the hospital and had a miscarriage. I was so surprised that he broke down crying. He was on his knees hugging me and touching my stomach.

"Why you ain't call me? I would have been there."

I just sat quietly thinking, *now this nigga wanted to cry for me, but he wasn't crying when he was fucking his baby's mom and getting her pregnant.* Why didn't he just marry her ass instead of me? Gina came back downstairs with her arms folded and stared at me like she was waiting for an explanation. "What? Why you keep on staring at me?" I asked clearly sounding irritated.

"Where have you been? You look a mess, and I didn't raise you like this."

She didn't raise me at all, so I didn't know what she was talking about. Gene walked over to her and told her about the miscarriage. She looked at me and sucked her teeth. She knew I was lying. I had learned everything I knew from her. She didn't say anything. She just went into the kitchen. Gene convinced me to come home with him, and for the next couple of weeks, I barely said two words to him.

About a month after being home, I reached out to my brother Ronnie aka Rhonda, and he was so happy to hear from me. I was telling him how miserable I was and how I wanted to move. He told me how popping the ATL was and that I should come visit to see if I wanted to stay. I didn't need a visit to know that I wanted to stay. Hell, I *needed* to stay. He hadn't been talking to Gina much after the switch, and he swore he wouldn't say a word. I was headed to the ATL baby, and I probably wasn't coming back. What did I have to lose? Gene? Yeah right. He was never mine in the first place. Rome? He didn't even like me. Gina? I didn't give a fuck about leaving Gina. My life was messed up mostly because of her. Daddy? I would miss daddy, but I thought I could just go and get my life together, and then I could send for daddy and Rome and leave Gina by herself. So, I had nothing to lose.

I was headed to the ATL on the next thing smoking. I was just going to leave and not say a word to Gene. I packed my bag with about two weeks of clothes and loaded the Navi up with everything I could fit in it. I wrote a long letter to Gene, this time telling him it was over and that I was not coming back ever. I was headed to Hotlanta baby. I was going to go and work my tail off and get my own hair salon. Everyone up north went to the south and made it. I stopped by Gina's to say bye to Rome and daddy. Of course, Rome really didn't care that I was leaving. He was always with Gina anyway, so I would come back for him once I got myself together. All I needed was about ninety days.

As expected, Gina was discouraging. She told me how I would be back and that I would never make it, because I was too stupid to take advantage of all that I had to offer. She reminded me that I wasn't street smart. I wasn't too dumb considering how I had managed to avoid getting caught up with P. On top of that, I managed to set Draya and Mike up without anyone finding out. So, I was pretty damn street smart whether she knew it or not. I was going to Atlanta regardless, and I was going to make it. Daddy just kissed me and told me to always remember that I can do anything if I just believed. I hadn't heard him talk like that in years. I felt a little emotional when I hugged him, but I just brushed it off, hugged Rome, and ran out the door.

I was ready for my twelve-hour trip. I had snacks and a full tank of gas. I was headed to Highway 95 south, and Ronnie was waiting for me. He and I weren't as close as I was with Tim, but he was a girl now, so maybe he could be my big sister. I figured we could go shopping and do all the things I always wanted to do with Gina. By the time, I got to VA, I was already tired and didn't have good service on my phone. I made it to North Carolina and stopped in a small town to spend the night, so I could be refreshed for the rest of the trip. I remember clicking through channels and writing a list of goals for my life in Atlanta on the small note tablet that they had next to the bible. I remembered hearing one of those TV pastors saying to write the vision and make it plain and that's just what I did. The number one thing I was going to do was get my own salon. Then, I would get my own place and daddy and Rome could come. All I needed was a few months down there. I was going to save them and finally live a normal life.

I got up bright and early the next morning and hit the road out of the small town. I was in the ATL before noon, and I was so happy. Moving to Atlanta was going to make my life so much better. The city was amazing with tall buildings kind of like Philadelphia but not as big as New York. I recall stopping at a gas station not knowing that I had to pump my own gas, and a nice man volunteered to do it for me. This was not New Jersey at all. Everyone was so hospitable. I could definitely get accustomed to this, and the weather was so beautiful. I pulled up to what looked like a mansion to me at the time. Shit, it was definitely a mini mansion. I was thinking to myself, *this cannot be where Ronnie stays. There is no way he stays here.* I had to go through a gate to get into his community, and there was a pool and tennis courts for the recreation of the community's residents. There was no way black people lived like this.

I was literally astonished as I pulled into the driveway. Jerome's parents had a nice house, but it had nothing on this house. To my surprise, a woman came to meet me outside and she was stunning. I had to do a double take, because *she* was Ronnie. He looked just like a woman from the nails that were freshly polished with a French manicure to his boobs that were sitting up perfectly. The red heels he had on were to die for. He hugged me so hard. The last time I saw him, he did not look this much like a woman, and he surely didn't have boobs. Where the hell did he get boobs from? He was on some other shit. He was a woman. He helped me get some stuff out the car and strutted down the cobblestone walkway to the front door.

Before we went in, he whispered in my ear, "I am Rhonda now. So please refer to me as Rhonda, and we will be A-OK."

That didn't bother me at all. Hell, he looked more like a woman than I did. When I walked in, I immediately looked up at the high ceilings that I now know were cathedral ceilings. I mean this place was something out of a magazine.

"How the hell do you afford this, boy - I mean, girl?"

"I'm a working girl," she replied.

I got even happier, because if Ronnie could do it, I knew I could. He walked me around the place for a quick tour. There was one room downstairs and four upstairs. The kitchen was huge, and the backyard had a huge deck. He gave me the bedroom downstairs which was fully furnished. All I had to do was move in because it was perfect. We sat down to catch up, and I told him about everything that was going on with me and how grateful I was to be there. He called Gina and told her I was safe, but they didn't talk long. I was not trying to talk to her negative ass. Gina apparently didn't know Ronnie was living like that, or she would have said something. She no longer treated him like her precious son since he decided to live life as a woman. If only she could have seen him.

After I sat talking to Ronnie for about two hours, two men walked in the house. One was clearly gay and the other was not. He introduced me to his roommates. Savion was the gay one and the other guy was Chuck. They both were very attractive but Chuck more so - maybe because I knew he wasn't gay. Savion was from Puerto Rico, and he had a very thick accent.

"You like chicken and rice, mami?"

I just nodded my head yes.

"You beautiful, girl. Rhonda, why no tell us you have such a beautiful sister?"

Ronnie just laughed. We all sat in the kitchen waiting for Savion to finish cooking, and it was smelling so good in there. We ate out back on the deck and just talked, drank wine, laughed, and enjoyed each other's company. It felt so refreshing. Gene had not even called my phone to see if I was safe, but I really wasn't concerned with him anyway. I just wanted to start my life in Atlanta. I remember falling asleep laying on my big sister's shoulder. She was exactly what I needed at that time. I needed love. The next few days were so much fun. Chuck was not home as much as Savion. Savion and I started to form a bond. We would all go on shopping trips and go out to eat. We were a family. I didn't even call back home to check on Rome because I knew he was okay as long as he was with Gina.

One night after Savion and Rhonda went to sleep, I stayed up watching the news. I always liked to know what was going on in the world. Chuck came in kind of late, and we sparked up a conversation. He was so nice and friendly. He was born and raised in Atlanta. Rhonda's house was not in the city of Atlanta but on the outskirts known as the metropolitan area. He explained to me how he grew up in the hood and with his grandma in the projects. I didn't even know Atlanta had projects. His conversation was intriguing and very funny with this crazy southern accent. It was kind of cute.

We talked until the sun came up, and then he kissed me on the cheek and went upstairs to bed. I did wonder at the time what in the world a handsome guy like him was doing in the house with a gay man and a transgender. Although, he didn't know Rhonda was Ronnie, but I didn't read too much into it. Savion went to the kitchen and started breakfast. He was a great cook. I was telling him about how I wanted to open a salon, and he told me about wanting his own restaurant. Then, he threw me for a loop.

"So, are you going to start escorting like me and Rhonda?"

I looked at him with a very confused face because I didn't even know what escorting meant.

"What is that?"

He explained how you go on dates with guys for money. They paid you just to hang out with them. It sounded crazy to me.

"You mean to tell me that all you have to do is spend time with them?"

He assured me that was all.

"Hell yeah where do I sign up?"

Just then, Rhonda came downstairs with her usual flamboyant self. She was always over the top. She had a full face of makeup and her hair was already curled. She had the best weave I had ever seen. Savion began to tell Rhonda what he'd just told me about the escort business and that I wanted to do it. Rhonda looked surprised that I wanted in, but I was happy to be in Atlanta and now to have a job. Rhonda explained that the fee for one hour was $125. Since she was doing all the setup, she would get $50, and I would get $75. That was cool with me because I could go on at least three dates a day. Breakfast, Lunch, and Dinner. No problem. So this is how they made money. It was a good business and I was ready to jump in head first.

Savion helped me pick out some outfits while Rhonda began to search for some dates. She had a website and everything. Chuck woke up later that evening when I was getting dressed and sat on the bed and just talked to me. I did notice him staring at me, and I can't lie, I wanted him to look. I loved the attention that he was showing me. He said I looked nice, and he walked over to me, fixed my hair, and this time gave me a kiss on the forehead. I was ready to make my first $75. Chuck said he would drive me, because he wanted to make sure the person wasn't crazy. I was cool with that. I was actually meeting the guy at a hotel, and we were going to have room service. His wife had died, and he just wanted the company. I for sure could do that. Chuck said he would wait since it was only an hour. Rhonda made it clear that I was not to spend more than one hour with him.

I remember walking into this beautiful hotel and going to room 112. An old white man came to the door. I was a little surprised to see that this was my date, but it didn't bother me. He looked really nervous, but I wasn't. I just started talking and drinking. He did have some snacks, but it wasn't dinner. I just wanted to get the $125 and get the hell out of there, so I could get to my next $125. He sat on the bed and motioned for me to come over to sit next to him. I did without hesitation. After about ten minutes, he took my hand and placed it on his dick. I could barely feel it. I quickly snatched my hand back.

"What the fuck are you doing? This ain't that type of party." He pulled out the money and handed it to me, then dropped his pants and tried to push my head to suck his dick. I had no idea what was happening, and I just wanted to leave, but I was scared. I just stood there in shock like I had at the top of the stairs that day Tim died.

"Ms. I just want some head. I cum really fast," he said as he stroked his nasty old dick.

I just looked at him. I couldn't move. What had Ronnie gotten me into? I wasn't a damn prostitute... then it hit me that escorting was a fancy name for prostituting. I instantly remember that movie where the lady was a high class prostitute, but they called it escorting. I couldn't turn back since I was already there. I kept thinking, *what if he tried to kill or rape me.* If I just sucked his dick real fast, I could get out of there. So, that's just what I did. It was the slowest sixty seconds I ever experienced. As promised, he came fast and he even gave me an extra $50. I ran out the door so fast and rushed back to the car. Was I supposed to be doing this? Did Chuck know what was going on? He couldn't have? He just drove me. I surely wasn't going to tell him. I hopped in the car.

"That was fast." I just nodded my head and didn't talk the rest of the ride. When we got home, I ran to my bathroom to brush my teeth. I had never sucked a white man's dick, and I never wanted to again - especially not for money. There was no way I could do this. I went straight to Savion and told him what happened. He just started laughing.

"We all had that feeling our first time. You'll get used to it. You just made $75 for 60 seconds. Girlllll, this is the life."

It just didn't feel right. I began to think about Gene and how I was still his wife. I wanted to go home back to New Jersey. I did not sign up for this. I rolled my eyes and went straight to my room. Rhonda came in, hugged me, and explained that she thought I knew what I was getting into and that if I wanted to stop, she completely understood. I was so happy she said it, because I did want to stop. I wasn't strong enough to be a prostitute. I mean, I wasn't walking the street, but it was the same thing. Getting money for having sex with random dudes. Chuck came in the room and asked Rhonda to leave so we could talk. He started making jokes, and I was actually laughing. He was the funniest guy I had ever met. At the time, I didn't think he knew what was going on and I was glad. I laid down, and he laid next to me. He held me in his arms and did not try to have sex with me. We slept like that all night. It was so refreshing after I had just been misled into sucking some random man's itty bitty penis.

I woke up in Chuck's arms and couldn't understand why I was so comfortable laying with another man so shortly after leaving my husband. I guess it was because, he hurt me, and even if he didn't know about it, maybe I still felt like I was getting him back some sort of way. I moved his arm from around me and went in the living room and realized that Savion and Rhonda were gone. The car was not in the driveway. I sat on the back deck just listening to Mother Nature and wondering how I got dealt the cards that I was dealt. I know I had been promiscuous, but I never wanted to be a prostitute. I just wanted to open up my own hair salon, marry a man that loved me, be a good mom to my son, and live the American dream. I started to think this was not going to happen.

Chuck came out back, kissed me on the cheek, and brought me some orange juice. I don't know what it was about him, but I felt so comfortable talking to him. He was so down to earth. I was sharing with him the story about Gene and his baby's mom and how I had a miscarriage and Gene wasn't there so I was alone. I knew I was lying, but I wanted him to feel sorry for me. I made a rash decision to just walk up to him and kiss him, and he kissed me back with passion. We got it in right there on the back deck. It was very spontaneous. By this time, I had so many sexual experiences that I wasn't really fazed by any, but overall it was good. He was smiling and making jokes as we laid in the hot Georgia sun butt naked on the deck. Well, I still had my panties on, he just pushed them to the side. The incident from the night before had slipped my mind, and I was happy to be in his arms.

We went back in the house and I got dressed. I decided I was going to put what happen the day before behind me and go to every salon to see if I could get a job. I had to start somewhere. He stayed behind. I made my way to the downtown Atlanta area and put in an application at every salon there was, praying to get a call back. I was ready to start making my dreams come true and prostitution was not one of them. I stopped off to eat and wondered what life would be like with Chuck. He was nice and funny, and he would make a great husband, but I first had to divorce the husband I had. He still hadn't even tried to call to check on me. I got back home kind of late. I walked in and the house was very quiet I looked out back to see if anyone was there but no one was. I called out, *Hey y'all,* but no one said anything. I walked upstairs to see if I could find everyone.

Savion's room door was locked. He was like an old man who went to bed extra early. I walked to Chuck's room, but it was empty. I busted open the door to Rhonda's room to find Chuck doggy-style behind Rhonda.

"What the fuck are you doing?!" I yelled.

Rhonda jumped up, and I could clearly see his dick, so I know Chuck could see it, too.

"You know she's a man, and you still fucking her? Oh my God! I gotta get the fuck outta here," I said as I exited Ronnie's room.

Chuck just looked at me with a blank stare as Rhonda scrambled to put on some clothes. I ran downstairs to get my stuff and get the fuck out of there.

"Brea! Brea, wait! Brea, I wanted to tell you."

She began to explain how Chuck was her pimp, and he wanted us all to be a family. She had been fucking Chuck, and Chuck had been fucking Savion as well. She didn't mean to hurt me, but this was the life she lived. No one meant to hurt me, but they all managed to do it so well. I didn't say another word. I just cried and packed. I still had enough money to get back to New Jersey, and I was leaving immediately. She begged me to stay and with all the commotion, Savion woke up.

"Brea, honey this is life. It's really not that bad, and we making so much money," Savion said in his Puerto Rican accent as he tried to make me feel better about my discovery.

They had to be joking. I could not believe that I came all the way to Atlanta for this shit. I packed fast.

As I was leaving, I heard Chuck say, "Let her leave. We can't force her to get money. Let her go back to the hood."

I couldn't believe it. As I hopped in the truck, Rhonda ran to the car, and I rolled down the window.

She whispered, "I love you, baby sis. I'm sorry. I'm just so fucked up. Be safe."

She blew me a kiss as I hit the sidewalk with my back tire, trying to get the fuck out of dodge. That was the last time I would see her alive. I started to believe Gina had put a root on me. She was always right. I was the dumbest bitch alive. I was a lost cause. With this bullshit, I just needed to go home, be Gene's wife, let him cheat on me, and live unhappily ever after. I didn't know what was going to happen, but I was on Highway 85 North headed home. I wasn't going to ever discuss what happened in Atlanta with anyone. It would be added to my long list of secrets. I ripped up the paper that contained my list of Atlanta dreams and threw it out the window. I was tired of dreaming. FUCK dreams. Mine didn't come true.

Chapter 9 - Jerome is home

I had been back at Gina's for about a month and heard not one word from Gene. Gina said he came by, dropped my stuff off, said he was moving, and left. He didn't even care that I had been gone. No one seemed to care. When I first got back, Gina kept on prying me for information about Ronnie aka Rhonda and asking why I came back. I just ignored her. Rhonda kept calling me, but I would not talk to her. I kept myself locked up in my room. I barely ate, and I was becoming more and more depressed. Rome and I didn't have a real relationship. He didn't really want to be around me, because I was mean to him. He loved his Gina, and I was like a third wheel when they were together. Daddy didn't really talk too much, and it looked like he aged about ten years although I wasn't even gone that long. Gina would be the death of that man for sure. She was looking older too, but she was still fabulous - looks wise anyway. She was still a drunk pill popper though.

I tried to just stay out of everyone's way. I felt like a total stranger in my own parents' home. I really didn't even want to be there, but it looked like I had no other choice. I did manage to watch Rome play the game every now and then. I was trying to be some sort of mother to him. *Trying* is the operative word. The time had arrived for Jerome to graduate college. I could not believe he was graduating already. It had been many years since he and I had been involved, but I was happy for him nonetheless, and he was a great father to Rome. His parents would always get Rome, come to his sporting activities, and help financially. They were good people. Gina, Daddy, and Rome went to Jerome's Ivy League graduation. He did some kind of joint program where he got his master's and bachelor's degree at the same time. He was always smart.

His parents were throwing a big graduation party for him, and we all were invited. I did not want to go at all. I never loved Jerome, and I was not on his level. He never really was the bad boy, and I guess you could say I was the bad girl that liked bad boys. Being around him and his family made me feel so uncomfortable. So, I decided to just stay home and soak in all my guilt, shame, and depression. After the party Gina, Daddy, and Rome came home with a bunch of food, and I had finally worked up enough hunger pains to eat. I made sure everyone was sleep before I went to the kitchen and loaded up my plate with the leftover BBQ and amazing pound cake that Jerome's mom made from scratch. I grabbed the hot sauce and a paper towel and headed upstairs.

When I got to the room, Rome was in my bed with a movie. I just smiled and told him to put it in. I never really hugged or kissed him or showed him any kind of affection, so it was kind of weird having him lying in my bed to watch a movie.

"Get on the floor, boy. Ya ass don't need to be in the bed with me. You too damn big."

He looked confused and hurt, but I ignored it and kept watching the movie. After the movie, he was telling me about his dad and how he was going to live with his daddy real soon. He said his daddy was going to get married and how pretty his dad's girlfriend was and that I would get him on the weekend. I had no idea where this was coming from all of a sudden. Married? When did Jerome get a girl? Everyone knew he was waiting for me to settle down. Nonetheless, I was still listening to all he had to say. I was drilling my son to give me detailed information about who was at the party and about his dad's girlfriend. I could tell he was tired of telling me stuff over and over again, but I kept pushing for information. Finally, he just looked at me and ran to his room. This was probably the most I had talked to him ever, and all I could think about was what the hell Jerome was doing. It was like I had a one track mind. I knew in order to get some answers, I would have to call Jerome myself. I played him so many times, but he could never get enough of Brea, his one and only true love.

The next morning, I got up early to call him. I knew his parents would come get Rome for church every Sunday morning. I figured he was going with them, so I wanted to catch him before they left. I hadn't talked to him in probably over a year. Gina usually handled anything concerning Rome with him and his parents. I still decided to call and just thought he would be happy to hear my voice. I made small talk and asked him could we talk about Rome face to face. He quickly agreed, and I was ready to get to the bottom of this girlfriend thing. We agreed that I would come to his parents' house because they would be at church. For the first time in over a month, I got in the shower, did my hair, and put on some makeup. His parents had already picked Rome up for church.

As I walked downstairs, Gina and Daddy were sitting and watching the news. They both looked shocked to see me up and looking half way decent.

"Good to see you looking good, baby girl. You look so adorable."

Daddy always made me feel like a little girl. Gina looked me up and down and rolled her eyes.

"I'll be right back. I'm going to meet Jerome so we can talk."

Gina quickly jumped down my throat. "Talk? Talk about what? Don't you ruin that boy's life, Brea, with your slutty ways. He has a degree and he needs a good woman not like you."

She often had a way of crushing my spirit. Daddy patted her on the back and pulled her back as she had been on the edge of the couch by this point. I just rolled my eyes and walked out. I didn't have any expectations in going to meet him. I guess I just wanted answers from Jerome himself. I pulled up, and he was waiting for me outside. He had the biggest Kool-Aid smile on his face. I jumped out the truck, and he grabbed me and hugged me with my feet dangling off the ground. I don't remember Jerome being so tall and so damn handsome. The boy was no boy. He was a man, and he was fine. He grabbed my hand and guided me into the house. I hadn't seen him in so long besides glimpses of him when he was dropping Rome off. To be honest, I never really looked at him the way I was looking at him on this day.

We sat in the his dad's office, and he began to tell me about his college experience and how happy he was because he just got some corporate job with a Fortune 500 company. I didn't even know half the shit he was talking about. We had nothing in common, not even Rome since he was Vick's son. Why was I there? He was so intelligent, but I still didn't love him although I had love for him. I began to tell him about some of the things that had happened to me such as the break up with Gene and my fake miscarriage. He hugged me and told me that life would get better if I just believed that it would get better. I told him about what Rome said about him getting married. He just laughed and told me that he had a girlfriend, but marriage was not on his radar and that his parents had probably put that in Rome's head. We both laughed and enjoyed the moment.

He was always a great guy. I knew he was too good for me though. I didn't deserve a well-rounded man like Jerome. Besides, I was still married, so I just let that dream stay in my head. We talked for about four hours, and before we knew it, his parents were coming in from church with Rome. I knew we had to have talked a long time, because his parents went to a Pentecostal church and they went all day long. Rome ran in and stopped when he saw me.

"What are you doing here, mommy?"

Rome's parent were looking at me with disgust.

"Just talking to your daddy, but I'm *leaving now*" I replied as I stressed the "leaving now" part.

Jerome's mom looked at him with the most evil look. I really didn't understand why they hated me so much. I was always nice to them, but I guess they too didn't want me to influence him negatively. Jerome gave me a big hug and kissed me on the cheek. I gave Rome a high-five and said goodbye to his parents. I left with mixed emotions wondering what it would be like to be with Jerome. I was wondering if I could fall in love with a man like that.

Moreover, I was wondering how I could not fall in love with a man like Jerome. Then, I snapped out of it, because my dreams did not come true, ever. When I got to my parents' house. Gina was waiting for me drunk.

"Brea, why you such a slut? Why you gone mess up that boy life 'cause you messed yours up?"

One day I was going to tell that bitch off, but that wasn't the day. I just walked past her, brushing up against her flowery house dress and went straight to my room. About five minutes later, she came upstairs and handed me the phone. It was Jerome.

"Brea, I know you may not believe me, but I love you. I have always loved you. Do you want to try and to make it work?"

My mouth dropped open. I couldn't believe that he wanted to make it work with me. I quickly said yes without giving it any thought. I was so happy, but I had mixed emotions. I was still married and didn't know how to make anything work, but I still agreed.

"I'm coming to get you," he said before he hung up. I ran downstairs and daddy was in the kitchen.

"Hey, Daddy. What you doing?"

He just looked at me and hugged me as he said, "Brea, I love you, and I'm sorry for any pain that I may have caused you. I know you haven't had the perfect life, none of us have, but just know I love you."

Why was he saying this to me? I had the weirdest emotion come over me and tears streamed down my face. Many people had done me wrong, but none were ever sorry. Daddy was sorry, I could feel it.

"Daddy, I'm good. Don't get all emotional. Everything is fine," I said trying to force a smile.

He didn't say another word. He only kissed me on the forehead. I ran out the door and waited patiently for Jerome. I saw him coming, so I ran off the steps and forgot to close the gate. He kissed me as soon as I got in the car. We went to the local park and made out. We didn't have sex, but we had a lot of foreplay. I was glad he didn't try to have sex with me, because I really didn't want to have sex if I could help it. He just went on and on about how he loved me and how he was going to make me happy. He told me that he broke up with his girlfriend because he knew I was the one. It was all so overwhelming, and to be honest, all I could think about was my daddy apologizing to me.

He was so wrapped up loving me that he didn't even realize that the feeling was not mutual, but I just let him have his moment. He planned out our future, and I agreed with all he was saying. I just was not into him like he was into me. It was not the love connection I was looking for. We talked about how we could get Rome fulltime and get a house. I could be a stay at home mom, and we could have a little girl, too. It was all some shit I was just making up. Just to see him happy was great, because he deserved it but not with me. I had manipulated this man into sex as young teenagers knowing that I was having sex with other people and that my son wasn't even his. I had so many emotions. We spent most of the night talking and making out, and he finally took me home. I told him not to say anything to anyone about our relationship just yet, as I needed to handle my divorce from Gene and didn't want his parents to snap until I had my situation handled. He agreed. I laid in the bed wondering what life would be like if I just accepted that Jerome loved me, and if I could really make an effort to love him back. Life would be great, so that's what I was going to do, or so I thought.

Jerome and I began to date for the next few months and everything was actually pretty. I even landed a job as a receptionist. That was cool for now, because with Jerome on my side, I was determined to get my own salon one day. Gina and Jerome's parents knew something was up with us. I even went to church with them most Sundays. I filed for divorce and sent the papers to Gene's last known address. The attorney said as long as he didn't respond in within eighteen months, I could easily get a divorce under the terms of abandonment. One day as I was headed to work, I saw a black car parked up the road from Gina's house. I was very observant of strange cars. I had always wondered if P would jump out on me one day. Well, it was not P, but it was my husband, Gene. I hadn't seen his ass in months, and he was there looking at me like nothing ever happened.

"Get in the car, Brea. This will only take a minute."

I hopped in the two-door black Lexus coupe. It looked like the boy Gene was doing well for himself. I instantly went in on him about not calling me while I was in Atlanta, but he quickly shut me down.

"Brea, I fucked up and I want us back. I took the paternity test for that baby, and it ain't mine. I want you back. No bells. No whistles. Just you, me, and our love for each other."

It was not very romantic, but I was happy to see him and at least hear him out.

"We been through a lot from Kia to that Mike shit. I say we put it behind us and just move on."

He made it clear that he was not giving me a divorce. I told him that I was headed to work, and he quickly said quit that shit. He was a man of many words. I didn't quit, but I didn't call out either. I drove the truck to follow him to his place. Of course, it was out of the city. It was a very nice high-rise building with mostly white people. We walked into an amazing unit, and we were at it instantly. I mean, we had sex all over the place, and by the way he came all inside of me, I could tell he missed me. He went straight to sleep, and I began to play private detective. Here was my one track mind again. I had forgotten all about Jerome just that fast. I could only live in the moment. He didn't have much in the apartment. It was very nice but boring. Black this, black that. It was obvious that no bitch lived there. I could see myself living there with my husband, and we could be one just like I always wanted. What about Jerome? I'd figure it out later.

He had mirrors all over the apartment and began to look at myself and cry. I was an emotional mess. I went to the freezer, because I knew Gene always had some kind of liquor in there. He damn sure had some vodka, and I drunk it straight out the bottle. I was so overwhelmed by the constant changes and heartbreaks in my life. Gene woke up to me crying hysterically and hyperventilating. He was so freaked that he called 9-1-1, and he didn't fuck with the police. I was rushed to the closest emergency room and could tell he was really scared. He was holding my hand, but I was so out of it. The nurse came to draw blood from me, but my veins were so small that they had to use the little butterfly needles typically used on babies. I remember seeing that needle when I was pregnant with Rome.

Finally, I felt normal again after they gave me some kind of sedative. My heart wasn't racing and my breathing was stabilized. Gene held my hand and I laid on that cold hospital bed in that cold room. He kept saying how much he loved me, and I could feel it. The doctor finally came in and asked what my symptoms were. I told him how I always felt anxious and depressed for many years and how I was in heavy therapy as a child. He diagnosed me with depression and anxiety and gave me a prescription for Lexapro. He also gave me a follow-up doctor's contact information. I left the hospital feeling very broken and confused. That was my regular mood since I'd left Atlanta. I just couldn't function.

We went back to Gene's place after leaving the hospital. We were both silent and didn't say much. After a day of rest at Gene's house, he finally took me back to Gina's. Jerome was there when I got home. Gene would not let me walk in alone. He was determined to explain what was going on with me to my family. I begged him not to, because I knew that Jerome was inside, and I didn't want anybody to be hurt. We walked in and Jerome instantly grabbed me into a tight hug. He was clearly concerned. Gene pushed him away from me. Jerome looked at me, and I looked down to the ground. `

"Listen. Brea is sick y'all, and we're back together. So I'm going to help her get better," Gene said as he and Jerome had a stare-down. I hadn't even noticed that Mark was there as well. Mark didn't care for Gene, so he was looking at him with disgust. Jerome jumped in Gene's face.

"Look, homeboy. Brea and I have a son, and we're working it out. So, just be gone."

Gene just laughed, and I didn't say anything, because I didn't know what to say. Gina started screaming for me and Gene to get the fuck out of her house. Rome was crying because of all the commotion. Daddy was grabbing Gina, Mark was grabbing Jerome, and I was grabbing Gene to leave out the door. Gene was fired up talking shit when Mark hauled off and knocked him out. He just walked up to Gene and sucker-punched him. Jerome was hype, too. I was trying to calm everyone down. Gene finally regained consciousness, and I was helping him get out the door. Jerome stopped me as Gene and I headed out the door.

"This how you want it Brea? What happened to you and me? You said we were going to be a family. You said we would make it work. What about real love, Brea?"

Jerome had so much pain in his heart. I hurt that man so bad. I just kept walking out the door with Gene hanging onto me. I pushed Gene into the passenger side of his two-door coupe and jumped in the driver's side. As I drove back to his apartment that day, I knew I had made one of the worst decisions of my life. Gene was just happy because he had won, he wasn't happy that he had me back. He just wanted to control me, and that's just what he did. I could not get Jerome's words out of my head. *What about love?* Yeah, what about love, Jerome? It never really meant shit to me.

Chapter 10 - I Just Wanna Die

After the whole escapade with Jerome, I didn't want to talk to him at all. I was so ashamed because I had hurt someone that seemed to truly love me. I was getting really tired of hurting so badly inside, and the damn medicine that I got at the hospital was only making me more depressed. I continued to take it and just laid in the bed all day. I hadn't talked to Gina, Daddy, Jerome, or Mark for a few weeks now. I really wanted to see Rome. I wanted desperately to be a good mom to him. When Gene came home one day, I decided to tell him all that had happened to me in Atlanta. I told him the whole truth and about how I felt so crazy. He really didn't have anything to say besides how much I deserved that for leaving him. He even had the nerve to say that I should always stick by my husband no matter what. He didn't even try to console me. He always had a way of making it all about him. I don't even know why I told him.

After Gene left back out for his daily work as a hustler, I made a rash decision to call Gina. When she answered, I asked to speak to Rome. She didn't hesitate putting him on phone. I was shocked because I expected her to drill me. Rome came to the phone and I could tell he was out of breath from running downstairs. We talked for a while, and he expressed concern for me. Then he said something that made my heart drop. He informed me that his dad was getting married the following week. What the fuck! How could Jerome be getting married? I mean, he said he broke up with the girl. It had only been about three weeks since the big ordeal with us at Gina's house. There was no way he was getting married. After Rome and I finished talking, I hung up quickly before Gina could get on the phone and drill me. My mind began to wander and I called Jerome. I just picked up the phone and called him. He was not happy to hear from me, but I could hear the hurt in his voice.

"Look, I'm marrying my girl. We decided to make it work. Besides, she's more my speed, Brea, and I'm happy. Let me be happy."

I held the phone in silence, because he was right. I needed to let him be happy, but I knew he wasn't happy without me. I begged him to come over since I knew Gene wouldn't be back until the next day as usual. To my surprise, he agreed after I begged him for about thirty minutes. I jumped in the shower as soon as we hung up. I didn't take my "happy pill" as Gene and I called it, because I didn't want to be sleepy. I went to the freezer and pulled out the vodka and drunk about half the bottle. The doctor told me that I shouldn't drink while I was on the medicine, but I did not listen at all. Jerome arrived, and I was on my knees when he hit the door.

"Jerome, I'm sorry. Please forgive me. Gene is crazy, and he was threatening me."

I could tell he didn't believe me. As a matter of fact, I could even tell that he didn't want any parts of me. However, I was going to make him want me. Jerome had never rejected me and I wasn't going to allow him to start. After all, he was a man, and I knew how to get what I wanted from him. I walked up to him and started kissing his neck and grabbing his dick. It wasn't long before we were in the bed that I had shared with Gene. Strangely, before he was about to go inside, he pulled out a condom. What the fuck? I had never used a condom in my life, so I felt very offended that he had pulled out a condom to have sex with me. He explained that it wasn't me that he didn't trust, but it was my husband. After all the stuff I had told Jerome about Gene, I guess it was only right that he used a condom. Still, it made me feel like less of a woman. Why? I do not know.

While we were getting it in, I easily took the condom off, and there was nothing Jerome could or would do about it. It was just too good to him, and I knew that. There was no way I was going to let him not cum inside of me. That gave me some sort of satisfaction. After we were done, he was not happy about me taking the condom off, but there was nothing he could do about it at this point. Suddenly, he jumped up and told me we that couldn't see each other and that I needed to leave him alone. I knew he wanted to believe the words that were coming out of his mouth, but he didn't. So, I just let him talk and leave. Hell, I had got what I wanted. It actually felt good to be in control, and I knew that if I could control anyone, I could control Jerome.

Gene didn't come home that night which reminded me of the many nights I spent alone before I left for Atlanta. I wasn't surprised that he probably was still fucking Kia, but oddly enough, I really didn't give a fuck. I didn't give a fuck about much at that time in my life. He finally came home the next day like nothing ever happened. I was already very drunk, and it was early afternoon time. He fell straight asleep, and I went right for his phone. I never trusted that nigga after the bullshit he put me through. He had a lock on his phone this time, and I couldn't figure the shit out. I began to look all over the apartment to see if there was anything I could find. I was in the kitchen draws, the bedroom draws, the closets, and the spare bedroom. My search yielded nothing, but something told me go into the closet again. Bingo! I discovered a safe behind his many sneakers.

The safe had a password key pad on the front of it. He was knocked out on the bed, but I was still nervous to attempt to get in it. I decided to wait until he got up to leave before I attempted to break the code. Meanwhile, I started writing down multiple four-digit codes that could lead me one step closer to opening the safe. He woke up later that evening wanting to have sex with me. Of course I didn't want to, but I did because I just wanted him to leave me alone. After we fucked, he left just like I wanted, and I went straight for the closet. I tried birthdays, holidays, and last four digits of his social security number, and none of the numbers worked. Finally, something told me to try our anniversary, and it actually worked. I couldn't believe the nigga even remembered our anniversary, let alone set that as a passcode to his safe.

I opened the safe and found the divorce papers I had sent to him, money, diamond earrings, and a document from the Office of Paternity at the Camden County Courthouse. I read the document and saw printed within the first few lines: *Gene Davis you are 99.98% the father of said child Rachel Davis.* So, this muthafucker was the father of Kia's new baby, and he knew it. I also noticed that the divorce papers were open and there was no forwarding address. Therefore, he had to still have access to the place where he and I stayed before I moved to

Atlanta. I was not surprised, he had been a lying, cheating asshole since I met him. I don't even know why I chose to go back to his ass. I should have just stayed with Jerome and tried to make it work. I was so fucking stupid. As I sat there kicking myself in the ass, I made an impulsive decision, as usual, to go to the place where Gene and I lived together. Something just didn't feel right. I guess you could call it a woman's intuition.

I drove the long thirty-minute drive back to our old town. When I arrived, the old car Gene had and the new two-door coupe were both parked outside. What the fuck? If this nigga moved, why were both of his cars there? I had to think for a minute. Fuck thinking. I was going in. I walked to the door prepared to knock on it hard as fuck. However, before I began to knock, I remembered that I had a key. I was sure he had changed the locks, but I still tried multiple keys. Finally one of the keys unlocked the door. I slowly opened the door and creeped up the stairs. No one was in the living room. I took my four-inch stiletto heels off and walked slowly to the back bedroom. As I looked around, I saw a lot of baby shit like diapers, wipes, and clothes. There was also a bunch of alcohol on the table and some weed. I walked to the back bedroom and found my husband fucking none other than his dirty ass baby's mom. He loved that hoe. He was fucking that bitch with the baby that he said wasn't his laying right next to them.

Instantly, I jumped on both of them and started swinging. I hated that bitch. I honestly don't think I would have been as mad if it was a new bitch, but it was this bitch again. I was beating the shit out of him and her. I ran out the door with him chasing me with a blanket around him. I was beyond tired and beyond hurt. She had a nerve to be standing on the patio with no bra on screaming, "Let that bitch go." I was definitely going and for good this time. Gene tried to chase after me, but he couldn't catch me. There was so much glass on the ground and he wasn't wearing any clothes or shoes. I jumped in the truck and pulled off. "Bye Gene and good ridden." He just stood there holding the blanket with one hand in the air for me to come back. I didn't even cry I was so mad, but I was mad at myself.

I drove straight to Jerome's house and didn't care that I didn't call. His parents were big on respect and calling before coming to their house. That was all out the window. I was going to be with Jerome, even if it killed me. I knocked on the door and his mom answered but would not let me in the house. She explained the importance of calling first and that I just needed to leave Jerome alone. She said that he was moving on without me and that they did not want any trouble. I guess he didn't tell her that he had just been with me sexually. I left and called him from my cell phone. He answered and told me not to call him anymore and that he was getting married and wanted nothing to do with me. I went back to his parents' house, got out the car, and banged on the door.

I was frantically yelling, "Jerome, answer the fucking door you coward! Tell me to my fucking face!"

His dad came out, and he was not confrontational at all. He gave me a hug and told me to just move on with my life. I broke down crying, begging for Jerome to come out. He wouldn't come out. I went to Gina's only for her to ridicule me about how I messed up my life and how I was trying to mess up Jerome's life. I guess no one messed up my life in her eyes. I ran to the basement, but daddy was asleep. I ran upstairs and just cried my eyes out. I had that nasty cry with snot coming out my nose. I reached in my signature coach bag for my antidepressants and took two pills. I just remember laying on the floor hoping I was dreaming. Apparently I wasn't, because about three hours later, Rome was in my room telling me to wake up.

"Get the fuck out my room, yo! Leave me the fuck alone you annoying ass little boy!"

After he left, I began to cry again. I stayed in the room for five days straight, only coming out to use the bathroom. I think even Gina with her non-compassionate ass was starting to worry. Gene had been calling, but after Mark beat that ass up, he knew he wasn't welcome at Gina's house. I did get up on day six to brush my teeth and eat, then back to bed I went. Gina came and told me that Rome was going to be in Jerome's backyard wedding and I was not to interfere or they would call the cops. Why would she even tell me? She wanted to hurt me on purpose. I know she did. I just laid and cried every day for the next four weeks. I began to feel really sick. I mean extremely sick. Jerome was married, Gene was still a hoe, and I was back at Gina's. Three complete nightmares.

I was hoping that I was not pregnant, because that's exactly what it felt like. I managed to go to the store to get a test, and damn if it didn't say pregnant! It was either Gene's or Jerome's. I was so desperate for attention and affection. I called Jerome even though I knew he had gotten married just a few weeks prior. I begged him to meet me, and I told him I had some health issues. That worked, and he agreed to meet me but in a public place. I put the pissy pregnancy test in my purse and met him at the local store. I hopped in his car when he pulled up and showed him the test.

He was quick to say, "You were fucking me and your husband. How you know it's mine?"

I couldn't believe he was questioning me. I mean he was right, but how dare he question me. He refused to listen to anything I had to say and told me to get out his car. I was in so much pain, but I just got out of the car. Before I went back to Gina's, I called my last resort, Gene.

"Brea, baby let's talk."

I agreed and he met me around the corner from Gina's. I made him get in the car with me and I pulled out the test. He was not happy. He expressed his concerns for his many children and his new baby and that my pregnancy was not at a good time for him. He wanted to talk about us, but I wanted to talk about when I was getting my abortion, because I didn't want to be with his ass at all. He took me back to his apartment and tried to explain the whole baby thing and how he was going to tell me, but I wasn't listening. I just needed to schedule my fourth abortion, and I needed this nigga to pay for it and to be my driver. I didn't give a fuck what he was talking about with the being together bullshit. I made the appointment for the next week. I stayed at Gene's the entire time, but he wasn't even there. I didn't bother Jerome. I made up in my mind and promised God that it would be the last abortion I would have. I just needed to get my life right and fast.

The next week, Gene and I went to the same clinic that I had frequented many times. I was prepared to have my fourth abortion. I wasn't scared or nervous. I just wanted it to be over. Nothing had changed since the last time I was there except the nursing staff. They had the same chairs, same magazines, same protestors, same crackers, and the same me. After it was over, Gene tried his best to make me feel better. I guess he thought it was my first time at the rodeo. I was so unfazed. I was over it, I was over life, and I was over me. He left me at his apartment alone. I had taken my Lexapro to relax, and they gave me something for pain. I decided to take a few shots because my nerves were so bad. I cried constantly and took a note pad and began to write. It turned into a goodbye letter to everyone I knew. I just didn't want to live anymore.

I reached in the top of the closet looking for the .22 that Gene had for me in case of an emergency, but it wasn't there. I figured I could take the whole bottle of pills, but I already had the hardest time swallowing. I just threw the vodka bottle across the room. It shattered all over, leaving glass on the floor. Just then, it hit me. I could cut myself, but I wasn't strong enough to kill myself that way either. Damn, I couldn't even figure out how to kill myself. I was stupid as shit just like Gina always said. I finally decided the easiest way would be to take pills, so I took twenty Lexapro pills and drunk the rest of the vodka that was in the bottle. I didn't feel anything at first. I was already out of it from the abortion I had earlier that day. I remember feeling extremely tired and laying on the floor because the bed was too far away. I was laying in glass and all, but I didn't care. The next thing I remembered was being in the ambulance with Gene by my side and a fat white guy connecting stuff to me, but I could not move. I was dying, but I didn't really want to die. I just wanted to be loved and have a happy life. Why would I try to kill myself?

Chapter 11 - The Past in the Pulpit

I woke up in the hospital a few days later,
after being out of it from all the drugs I had
voluntary taken along with the drugs I was
involuntary given. When I finally regained
consciousness, I realized that Daddy was there, and I
could see Rome and Gina sitting on the sofa across
the room. Daddy reached in to kiss me, and his face
lit up. I could see the worry in his face. Daddy wasn't
really good at hiding his emotions. Rome came over
and hugged me. Gina didn't say anything. She just
kept looking down as daddy and Rome were talking
my ear off. I looked around for Gene or Jerome, but
neither were there. Rome managed to tell me that his
daddy was there but had to leave. However, no one
mentioned Gene, and I was too tired to talk to them.
Daddy took Rome to get something from the snack
machine.

At the same time, while he was gone, Gina began to talk to me.
She really was a demented bitch. She was shaking
really bad and pacing the floor. She wanted me to
explain why I would do this to her and embarrass
her in front of all those white people. The crazy thing
is that the doctor was black, the nurses were black,
and the guy taking the trash was black. So, I
couldn't find all the white folks she was talking
about. She was always talking about stuff that I
didn't understand at all. I was totally confused about
why she was drilling me about doing this to her,
when my attempted suicide would have no adverse
effect on her in anyway. I just let her make this
about her like she did everything my entire life. I

wondered why God had let me live. My life had absolutely no purpose. I was hopeless.

Gene came later that evening after Gina, Daddy, and Rome left. He came so late, because he said he didn't want to be bothered with my family. He looked like he hadn't slept well. He basically told me that we both needed to get ourselves together, so it would be best if I stayed at Gina's until we could "work things out." Whatever that meant. I know he thought I was crazy after I pulled a stunt like that, but I really didn't care what he thought. I was pissed at God for allowing me to live. I was pissed at the world.

They kept me in the hospital for a few days under suicide watch. They kept giving me these "crazy pills" as I called them, which didn't do anything but make me sleepy. About a day before I was to be released from the hospital, a counselor came to see me. I had seen many counselors before but this lady was special. First of all, she looked like me, and she was super intelligent. Gina seemed to hate white people, but she would always send me to one of those white men shrinks that didn't have a clue about my life. This lady was tall and brown-skinned with dread locks.

When she hit the door I could smell her perfume, and I could tell it was very expensive just by its pleasant fragrance. I was so impressed with her, and I hung on to her every word. I had never met a woman so classy and elegant that looked like me. She was not faking the funk. She asked me a lot about myself, but I never really answered her, and if I did, I wasn't honest. She was trying to get to the "root" of my problems, but I already knew the root of my problems and nothing could change that. Therefore, I saw no need to discuss it.

The day that I was released, the counselor, Ms. Warren was there when Gina came to pick me up. When Gina walked in and saw me talking to her, she looked very annoyed. I could tell by her demeanor. Gina always acted fake, but around this lady, Gina was acting nervous and jittery. She was intimidated by the lady, and I thought it was great to see that someone made Gina nervous. Ms. Warren made an appointment to come visit me two to three times a week until I felt better.

When Gina and I got in the car, she instantly start bitchin'.

"Brea, I hope you wasn't telling that lady all our business, because them people can't help you, girl. They gone put you in a crazy house, so you better act normal."

Too bad I wasn't normal at all. I needed the help. I assured her that I didn't share any family information with my counselor.

"I don't want that uppity negro at my house either, looking around judging us."

She just went on and on, and I tuned her out while I sat thinking of my next move. I was not going to be staying with Gina long. There was no way. Daddy and Rome had attempted to make me a cake, and it actually did put a smile on my face. I was very happy to see Rome, and I knew I needed to do better for him. He didn't ask to be born. Since I was his mother, I would see if maybe Ms. Warren would be able to help me. I didn't have anything to lose by seeing her, and the visits were free. The hospital set it up under some suicide prevention program.

Later that night, I wanted to call Jerome but didn't have the nerve, so I just didn't. I was not interested in calling Gene. He had hurt me so badly, and I was over being hurt. There was no one else to talk to, until Rome came into my room.

"Mommy, I pray you feel better. Gina said you were going to go to hell because you tried to kill yourself."

Why would this fucking bitch tell my child I tried to kill myself? This was exactly why I had to get the fuck out of there and fast. I just listened to him talk until I fell asleep on him. The next morning, I had a follow up appointment with Ms. Warren. I had called her that morning to see if I could meet her at her office, but she insisted that we go to a small restaurant not too far from the mall. That was fine with me, because I knew Gina would snap if I let her come to the house. I pulled up, parked, and waited for her. She pulled up in a navy blue Jaguar about fifteen minutes after I did. Classy was an understatement for Ms. Warren. I could see the dark tan leather seats through the windows of the car. I had seen a many fancy cars in my day, but it was something about a Jaguar that said class, especially with Ms. Warren jumping out of it.

She had to be around forty years old, and I didn't see a wedding ring, so I assumed she wasn't married. She strutted into the restaurant in her 6-inch heels with confidence all over her face. I rummaged through my dirty SUV looking for my Mac Lip Glass and fixed myself in the mirror. I finally went in, acting as if I had just arrived. She ordered a glass of red wine, and I followed suit. I really wanted some vodka, but I wanted to follow her lead. She began to ask me about myself. I just told her a generic story about school, being a teen mom, great parents, and the usual bullshit story I told everyone. She was not buying my bullshit.

"Brea, you have to be honest if you want to live a fulfilled life. You are beautiful and amazing, and God has huge plans for you if you would just be honest with yourself."

No one ever talked to me like she talked to me. She talked to me like she believed in me. It was crazy, because just by the few conversations I had with her, I really wanted to make a change. However, I still didn't tell her any of my personal business, especially about Tim, the set up with Draya and Mike, or the ordeal in Atlanta. I wasn't prepared to tell her all that. I just listened, and she invited me to church with her on Sunday. I was hesitant, but I decided that I would at least give it a try. She explained how her church was non-traditional, and I could even wear jeans. That was odd, because Gina's church was very conservative, and Jerome's church made the women wear long skirts. I was happy when she said I could dressed comfortably at her church. It was on! I would meet her at church the following Sunday.

That whole week, I was very happy about the future and what it had in store for me. I don't know if it was what Ms. Warren said or how she said it that had me on a high on life. I could not wait to go to church, and I was going to take Rome with me. That Sunday, I got up and changed about five times. I didn't want my shirt to be too low cut or my jeans to be too tight. I was so used to Gina criticizing me that I was very critical of myself. I finally decided on a turtle neck sweater with some dark blue jeans and ankle boots and a chain belt to finalize the look. Rome had been dressed for over thirty minutes waiting for me to come downstairs so we could go. As soon as I hit the bottom step, Gina came at me with her usual bullshit.

"What kind of devil church you going to with jeans on?"

She always had a way of putting a cloud over my sun or raining on my parade. I was already feeling self-conscious, but now my anxiety had heightened due to her comments. However, I was still going to church. I ran out the door with Rome tripping over his feet to follow me.

We arrived at church, and it was packed but not with the usual church goers. Mostly everyone was my age, and they all were dressed casually. I was so excited, because I had never been in a church like this. Maybe God did have something for me just like Ms. Warren said. The praise and worship service was awesome, and I even felt a few tears drop down my face. I wiped them quickly so no one would notice. I didn't want the usher rushing over with her box of tissues. Rome was in the children's section they had reserved in the back. It was finally time for the pastor to come, and man did they introduce him. I was sitting far in the back, because the church was jammed packed. When he got on stage, he looked so familiar to me, but I could not figure out how I knew him. I just sat back and enjoyed the service.

I remember him discussing forgiveness and God not judging for the things you had done. One thing he said stuck with me. You cannot change your past, but you can change your future. This was everything I needed to hear. I had found me a new church. Just then, he turned to thank his wife who happened to be Ms. Warren, or should I say Mrs. Warren. I was smiling so big, because I didn't know she was married. They had three children who stood up as well. *What a lovely family,* I thought. He opened up the doors of the church for people to join, but I was too scared to go up there. I really wanted to, but I just stayed seated. He did say that we could fill out a form to join church after service if we desired. He also invited all new visitors to stay so he could introduce himself.

After service, I went to get Rome from the back and then walked up front to say hello to Mrs. Warren and meet the pastor who delivered the most amazing sermon I had ever heard. I waited patiently, and Mrs. Warren quickly grabbed me and hugged me. I introduced her to Rome, and she was so happy to see us. She then went to introduce me to the pastor with such great enthusiasm.

"Honey, this is the beautiful young lady I was telling you about. Her name is Brea and this is her son Rome."

In that instant, the man turned to look at me and as he reached in to hug me, I could not believe my eyes. It was Vick, and he looked just like my son, or should I say my son looked just like him. What the fuck!? I hadn't seen him in years, since he left me hanging while I was pregnant. There was no way he could be Mrs. Warren's husband. Was Mrs. Warren the woman he left me to be with all those years ago? She was. He reached in and hugged me, and I know he knew it was me, but he still maintained his fake church smile. I was furious, but

I remained cool. He was talking to me, and he had a nerve to shake Rome's hand. His kids ran over, and one little girl had to be the around the same age as Rome. I almost died right there in the church. His church. Vick the big drug dealer from Philly was a Pastor.

I ended the conversation very quickly and got the hell out of that church. What was I going to do? No one knew about Vick but Tia. Did he tell his wife about me? How could I continue to see this great and powerful woman knowing that her husband is the father of my son? Rome looked just like him and his kids looked just liked my son. What the fuck was I going to do now? I was clearly upset, and Rome kept talking my ear off about how much he loved that church and wanted to go back and can we stop and get ice cream.

"Shut the fuck up! I can't think Rome."

He started his crying like he often did. He was such a damn cry baby. I couldn't get to Gina's house fast enough. I barely parked the car, and he ran in the house and slammed the door. I went in and went straight to my room. My heart was racing, and I was pacing the floor. How the fuck was Vick a pastor? What about his fucking son? He never even thought about us. I wasn't going to let that shit slide. This nigga wasn't shit. I needed a plan, and I needed it fast. I was scheduled to see Mrs. Warren in a few days, and I was going to go for sure.

This time we met at her office. It was a very small but nice office in the downtown area of Camden. I walked in with knots in my stomach. I did not know what he had told her, if anything. When I walked into the office, she hugged me and motioned for me to have a seat. She was so fucking classy. No wonder he didn't want to leave her all those years ago for me. We began to talk, and she was telling me how happy she was that I came to church and how God was going to begin to move in my life. Yeah fucking right. God didn't move in my life ever, but I listened as usual. Then, I flipped the script on her and started asking her questions. I could tell she was comfortable talking to me, because she began to open up about her life. She told me she just celebrated her tenth wedding anniversary. I was getting more pissed. Rome was almost nine, so this muthafucker was married when he was running up in house parties and taking trips to Atlantic City with my underage ass. Oh hell no. I tried to keep my composure, but it was hard. She began to sense something was wrong, but I just told her I needed rest and made a quick exit.

The whole ride home, I was determined to figure out how to handle this. I looked down and saw the program from the church service that I had attended. It read: *Pastor Victor Warren and Co Pastor Sharon Warren.* I let out the biggest scream and cry. I could not let Vick just live the fucking American dream. He needed to pay, and I had a plan that would get him to one way or another. I called down to the church the next day to schedule an appointment with good old Pastor Vick aka my real baby daddy. They scheduled me an appointment for the following day. I knew what I wanted to say and how I was going to handle it. I had my whole plan mapped out. The next morning, after filling out some job applications at a few temp agencies, I went over to the church for my appointment with the pastor.

When I walked in, he looked shocked to see me, because I gave a fake name.

"Well hello, Vick. Longtime no see."

He just dropped his head and started apologizing for his wrongdoings. He explained that he was young and that he really was in a different place. I wasn't trying to hear none of that shit. Nobody felt sorry for Brea, so I didn't give a fuck about Vick, and I was about to rock his world.

"I'm going to tell your wife everything. You broke my little heart all those years ago. I'm fucked up, Vick. I'm fucked up!"

I knew he would get nervous, because even if Mrs. Warren didn't believe me, I had my son as proof. He was begging and pleading because he had built a whole reputation in the community, and he didn't need this to come out, not now, not like this.

"What can you do to stop me? You abandoned me. I was only fifteen. You know that, right? I was fifteen when I had your son."

He looked confused, and think I fucked his head up even more, because he didn't know I was that young. He finally stood up and looked me in the eyes with tears rolling down his face. Now I had the power. I had shifted the energy.

"Would to take some money to never come into my life again, you know disappear?"

He really didn't even want to have a relationship with my son. You can say I was hurt, but I wasn't surprised. I threw out a number just to see what he would say.

"Give me $50,000, and I will leave you alone forever."

He made it clear that he could not move that much money out of the church funds to make that happen. He offered me $10,000, and I took it. My son didn't know this man anyway, and before that Sunday at church, I didn't even know if he was alive or dead. We shook hands on it, but we both had stipulations. I wanted the money the same day, or there was no deal. He agreed as long as I cut all ties from his wife and never came to the church again. He explained how his wife really liked me and wanted to help me, so I needed to stay far away from her. We shook on it, and just that fast, I made a deal with the devil.

He reached in the safe behind a painted picture of him and his family, minus Rome, and took out the $10k. This nigga really had $10,000 in a safe at his church. I just took the money and cracked a smile.

"You fine like wine back there Miss Brea," he said to me as I walked out of his office.

I just looked at him with disgust. Just like a nigga. Pastor or not, he was still a nigga, and he'd rather buy his way out of having a relationship with his son. That was cool though, because I had the $10k I needed to get the fuck out of Gina's house and maybe get a piece of mind. Mrs. Warren called me several times and even came by, but I had Gina make up an excuse. I guess she finally got the point, because she didn't bother me anymore after about a month of trying. I never went back to the church that had given me so much hope, and I never saw the lady that led me to the little sense of peace I had or to my past in the pulpit.

Chapter 12 – Well, Hello Mr. Officer

About three months after getting the payoff from Vick, I moved out of Gina's house. I didn't want her to get suspicious so I waited until I had a job. I had a really good job, according to Gina and Daddy, at a mortgage company working in the audit department. I was not making six figures or anything, but it was a decent job. Yet, it still was not the salon that I always wanted. I was taking my anxiety medicine on a regular basis, and I was feeling as close to normal as I possibly could. I had been spending more one on one time with Rome, but I still cussed him out every chance I got. I moved into a three-bedroom house not far from Gina, and I paid the rent up for six months with the money I had extorted out of Pastor Vick. It was a nice but small house, and it was all I needed. Rome was mostly with Gina, but he did come to my house more than he ever had in the past. It was just the two of us until I met Rudy.

After work I would hang out with a few coworkers at the local karaoke spot or somewhere for happy hour. I was really coming into my own and finding out who I was as an adult. I was finally enjoying life. One night while hanging out with my coworker Jessica, I met Rudy. Rudy was 6'7" with a caramel complexion, an amazing body, and beautiful teeth. He was talking to Jessica, but she had a man, so she really wasn't interested in talking to him. I really wasn't trying to meet anyone either. I was finally getting over Gene, and I had put Jerome out my mind because I didn't want to mess up his life more than I already had. Rudy walked up to me and introduced himself. He was very attractive and well-groomed. He dressed in a kind of nerd look, but I liked it. We talked for a while, and he told me he had a son who was ten years old. Rudy had never been married, and he was single. I was honest and told him that I was still legally married, but I did say that I was in the middle of a divorce even though I was not. Who knew when that was going to happen?

We exchanged numbers and began talking on a regular basis. He finally told me that he was a police officer which made me find him even more attractive. He was not the usual guy I talked to in the past. He was actually nice and very normal. We started dating, but I was determined to take it slowly. I was really trying to be a better person. I was still married and really wanted to divorce Gene, but I hadn't taken the steps to pursue it after I got out the hospital. I didn't want to mess this up with Rudy, because he seemed like a really good guy.

After dating for about two months, we decided to introduce our children to each other and they hit it off. They both loved wrestling, and they were around the same age. He would cook for me, and he was good at it and enjoyed doing it. He was extremely romantic as well. Everything was perfect in our relationship. I found myself not wanting to do anything but spend time with him. I was falling in love, and we hadn't even had sex. That was a first for me. I stopped taking my anti-depressants, because I felt like I didn't need them anymore. I was so happy and even the job was going great, although I didn't love it.

We began to frequent the local lounge where all the cops hung out. They were like a little gang, well more like a fraternity. I felt so comfortable there, and everybody was drunk and partying like crazy. I was drinking a lot this particular night and just dancing nonstop. Rudy was always talking and being social, so I just made my way to the dance floor alone. I started dancing with one of his colleagues, and we were having a good time. I could tell the guy was drunk, because he kept getting closer and closer and touching me a little bit. It was nothing out of the way and his wife was right there boosting him on. It was all in good drunk fun. Out of nowhere, Rudy came from behind me, grabbed me by my hair, and pulled me in the corner of the bar. It took the wind out of me, because I was not expecting that at all. He had me in the corner with his nails in my throat.

"Any woman of mine is not a whore. Don't ever disrespect me like that again."

He finally let me go, and I could feel the marks from his nails in my throat. I wasn't bleeding or anything, but I was so embarrassed, and the entire bar saw it. I just wanted to go home. I went into the bathroom, because I felt myself about to cry. I fixed my makeup and got myself together. The wife of the man I was dancing with came in the bathroom to check on me. I just laughed it off, but she did not find it funny. She let it go and told me to be careful. I just smiled at her and walked out of the bathroom. By this time, he was surrounded by his friends, and it looked like they were trying to calm him down. Soon after he walked over to me, gave me a kiss, and grabbed my hand while we walked out of the bar.

I was very quiet on the ride back to my place, because I was really hurting inside. It had taken the little bit of joy that I had back from me, but I was too hurt to even say anything. We arrived at my house, and he reached in and gave me the most amazing kiss before we got out of the car. Those butterflies that I had many years ago with Vick came back at that moment, even though he had just semi-choked me. He told me that he loved me for the first time and that he wanted me to move in with him. He said that he really wanted to be exclusive. I accepted not even considering myself or the fact that I had rent paid up for a few more months. I was thinking of stability. I mean, he didn't hit me, and it was just that one time. He had been the ideal man in those two months.

This night was a night for many firsts with us. We made love that night, and he was very gentle. He made sure I was okay, and he took his time. He made me forget all about the little incident we had back at the bar. Maybe he was just a little jealous. He stayed over, and that next morning I woke up to a full breakfast of steak, eggs, grits, and freshly squeezed orange juice. This made me extremely happy, and I fell deeply in love with this man. I moved into his place a week later, but I didn't let go of my place. I actually let my coworker Jessica sublease it, because the rent was still paid up for about three to four months. He had a beautiful house, and he made me feel so welcome. He treated Rome well too when he would come over. He even met Daddy and Gina, and she liked him. Gina never liked anyone. Rome even told his dad about how much he liked Rudy. We always did things with the kids.

We spent our first holiday together for Valentine's Day, and I was determined to get him a very nice gift. He worked a lot, and I really wanted to do something nice for him. I made a big dinner and had the house all laid out with rose petals. I wore the most amazing lingerie, and I was smelling amazing. The jacuzzi tub was going with bubbles foaming everywhere. When he walked in, I was going to blow his mind. I had the candles lit as I sat waiting at the table with my sexy robe open. He walked into the house and was visibly upset when he entered the dining room. I quickly jumped up from the table and went to hug him, but he pushed me away.

"Get this shit up, Brea. These rugs were imported, they are very expensive, and I don't need those red rose petals fucking them up."

He had a way of making me feel really low like Gina. I quickly began to pick them up, so we could be happy and enjoy the rest of the evening. He didn't like the rose petals and apparently not my outfit either, but I knew he would like the food. He went upstairs to take a shower, and I was trying to fix everything I had fucked up. He came back downstairs and began to eat. He was not happy and kept saying the food was cold and not seasoned well enough. I just sat there with my feelings hurt, because I didn't understand why he was so mad at me. I decided to just give him the watch I bought for him. He just said thanks and left out the door without saying where he was going. He just left me there alone on Valentine's Day. I tried calling him, but he didn't answer. I went upstairs and blew out all the candles I had lit and let the water out the Jacuzzi tub. I went into the room, took my lingerie off, and slipped on a t-shirt. Then, I cried myself to sleep, because I really didn't know what I did to upset Rudy. I started to talk myself into thinking it was all my fault until I finally fell asleep.

When I woke up the sun was up, but Rudy was not in the bed. I checked downstairs and in the kids' room, but there was no Rudy. I called his phone, but it was going straight to voicemail and the mailbox was full. I was beginning to worry, so I called out of work and got dressed. I continued to call him for hours, and he never called me back. Finally, he came home that evening knowing that he had to work the night shift. I was so upset and started cussing him out, because I was worried that something terrible happened to him. As I yelled and screamed, he continued to ignore me, and he was actually laughing at me. Without even attempting to tell me where he'd been and why he didn't come home, he just laid on the couch and went to sleep.

I don't know what made me do it, but I picked up his work boot and threw it right at his head and didn't miss. This naturally pissed him off and I ran while he chased me all over the house. He finally had me cornered as he towered over me while I squatted in a defensive position in the corner. He was so much taller than I was, which made me feel even more intimidated by him. He choked me off my feet and began punching me over and over again like I was a man. When he finally stopped punching me, he did the ungodly and spit on me before he walked away. I sat there on the floor crying, and he just went back to sleep. I could not understand where that sweet man went. He woke up later that evening, got dressed, and went to work without saying a word to me like I had done something to him. He was out all night, and then he had a nerve to come in and not explain. To make matters worse, he spit on me. I was not going to be treated like that.

When I went to work the next day, I was talking to Jessica and ended up telling about the night before. I usually didn't tell people my business, so I don't know what made me tell her. She was pissed and told me to come back to my house where she was living, but I didn't want to leave him. I just didn't want to fight with him. I tried to play it down like it wasn't that bad, but she knew it was bad and made it clear that it would only get worse. I couldn't help to think where he had been that night. It was Valentine's Day, and everyone usually was out with their mate, so where was he? I was determined to talk to him when I got home from work. He was sleep when I got there, but I decided to wake him up. He didn't get mad, and he actually was calm and willing to talk. He apologized for hurting me and promised to never do it again. I wanted to believe him so badly, but I just didn't know what to believe.

When he was punching me, it was like he was a different person. He acted like he hated me, so for him now to act like he loved me so much confused me. However, I was happy that he did say sorry, and we were moving forward. That weekend one of Jessica's cousins was having a party and she invited me to go with her. I wanted to go and hang out with them because most of my time was spent with Rudy since I'd met him. I told Rudy I was going to stay with Jessica because I didn't want to drive home drunk after the party, and I would come home the next morning. He seemed to be ok with that. Besides, he had to work the night shift anyway.

The party was fun, but I didn't drink too much, so I just decided to go on home. Jessica had a few people staying over, and I really just wanted to get in my own bed. I pulled up and noticed Rudy's patrol car out front. That wasn't odd since he was stationed not too far from where we lived. I walked in, but he wasn't in his usual spot in the kitchen or the couch. I didn't call his name just in case he was asleep. Sometimes he would come home and try to get a nap in because he worked so much. When I walked into the room, he is laying in the bed with a woman.

"Rudy, what are you doing?" I asked, hoping my eyes were playing tricks on me.

He had the nerve to look at me like I was bothering him. They were fully dressed in their uniforms, but she was laying in my bed watching TV with my man. If they were just hanging out, why was it in the room and not downstairs? She walked out of the room and her shoulder brushed up against my shoulder when she walked past me. Rudy got up and headed out of the room behind her, but I blocked the door.

"Rudy, what the fuck are you doing? You can't treat me like this."

He just laughed, but I would not let him pass me. I could hear the chick still downstairs like she was waiting for him. "You ain't going nowhere Rudy. Talk to me, please," I was so desperate for some type of explanation or even a bit of sympathy.

I got nothing. He was blank. He pushed pass me to go downstairs, but I ran after him. This bitch had a nerve to be sitting on the couch when we got downstairs.

"Get the fuck out, bitch. Why are you still here?"

She looked at Rudy, and he motioned with his head for her to go outside, and she did. He shut the door as she walked out, and then pulled out his police issued weapon that he was carrying on his hip. He was cussing at me about embarrassing him in front of his coworker, and he hit me right in the face with what felt like his fist. He hit me so hard that I literally saw stars, and I could instantly feel my eye swell up. I stumbled to the bottom step in an attempt to get my composure. He walked over to me, grabbed my hair, and put the gun to my head. I was crying hysterically.

"Bitch, don't you ever in your life question me about anything I do in my house. You do what the fuck I say! I don't do what you say! Just keep your mouth shut, and it will all be ok."

As soon as he walked out the door, I ran upstairs and looked in the mirror at my face. It was so fucked up, and I realized that he had hit me with the gun. There actually was a print from the gun on my face, and my eye was busted open and bleeding. I went downstairs and got a cold rag. My eye was burning and stinging, and it had completely closed up. I didn't know what to do or who to turn to for help. I grabbed the bottle of Hennessey he left on the counter and drunk the rest of it straight from the bottle. I couldn't call the cops, because he was the cops. I couldn't call Gina, because she would ask too many questions. I didn't want to call Jessica, because she would judge me. I could not believe he was treating me like this. Every time it seemed like my life was in order, it never was. I cried out to God for help, because I really needed it.

As I sat crying and praying, I saw a number come across the TV screen for a domestic violence hotline. I decided to call the 800 number to seek any type of advice or just for someone who did not know me to listen. Maybe God heard my cry. Maybe I had a way out somehow. A very pleasant lady answered the phone, and she listened to my story. I felt comfortable telling her the truth about the entire incident, and she assured me that she would help me. She advised me that someone would call me back in ten minutes with a meeting spot to take me to a safe haven. I wasn't too happy about going there, but I had to get the fuck away from him. I could see that relationship being the end of me. I quickly packed a small overnight bag and ran out of the house. I waited patiently at the gas station for the call back for my meeting place. I felt like I was on an undercover mission. Finally, she told me to drive to a hotel, and they would have someone escort me to the location. I thought this was the break I needed.

The lady on the phone talked about help with housing and jobs and even helping me get Rome back permanently. I always got myself into some bullshit, so maybe this was what I needed to work on me. I went to a local hotel to meet the escort for the safe haven. When I pull up, I saw a cop car, but I didn't think much of it because it was parked and empty. It was very dark and I could only see out of one eye. They called me to confirm that I was there and advised me to go inside because someone was waiting for me at the front. I put my shades on even though it was pitch black outside and slowly walked

into the motel lobby praying no one saw me. As soon
as I walked in, I saw Rudy waiting for me. I turned
around so fast and tried to make it to my truck. *How
did he know where I was? Was he following me?* He
ran and caught up to me. I was so scared that I
couldn't even get my keys out to open the door.

"Brea, you called the shelter. Don't you know
that the police escort women to the shelter? What the
fuck is wrong with you?"

He was my escort to the fucking shelter. There
was no way my luck could be this fucking bad. He
had me semi-pinned up against my truck, and he
pulled my glasses off my face and began to cry. He
went on about how he saw his dad kill his mother
when he was kid, and his dad got away with it
because he was only four at the time. He said that he
lost his temper, but he would never hurt me and that
I just needed to listen. He was crazier than I thought,
because he actually believed it was my fault. I was
so stupid and felt sorry for him, because he would
lose his job if I continued with the "domestic
violence" thing.

He was crying, and I believed he was sorry. He
was due to get off of work in the next two hours, so
he begged me to go home so we could talk. He said if
I still wanted to leave, he would let me go with no
issue. I wanted to make my life better, but I didn't
want him to lose his job. In addition to that, he
looked really sorry, and I really loved him, so I
decided to go back home. The lady from the shelter
kept calling me, but I didn't answer, and she didn't
even know my real name. I went home and waited on
the couch for him to come home.

When I woke up that morning, he was still not home. I called him, and he didn't answer. Finally, he arrived home reeking of beer. He was hugging and kissing me, and begging me not to leave. He promised to love me forever and never hit me again. I hugged him because I loved him more than I loved myself, and I wanted him to get better. He agreed to get some help, and then he attempted to have sex with me, but he was so drunk that he fell asleep in the middle of sex. I just laid there with him inside of me and sleep on top of me. I was praying that God would make him better. Unfortunately, he didn't get any better. He had actually gotten worse, and my dreams were nowhere near becoming a reality.

Chapter 13 – The Beginning of My End

I stayed with Rudy, and things remained the same despite his many promises. We were fighting almost every day, and he was for sure cheating on me in our house. I found condom wrappers, which we never used and underwear under my bed that were not mine. He was triflin', and he had no respect for me whatsoever, but I still stayed. He was even rude to Rome when he came over, so Rome began to stay at Gina's most of the time. I had lost my job due to the blow up we had after Jessica's party. I did a "no call/no show" because I was so embarrassed about my face, and they let me go. I still hadn't told anyone else the real deal, because I just didn't want to hear it. I needed to get a job so I could save up some money to leave him for good.

After a few weeks of looking, I landed a job at a collection agency. The pay was really good, but there was no room to grow. My dreams of having my own salon were fading away faster and faster each day I spent with Rudy. He made me feel the absolute lowest that I had ever felt. I was working close to Gina's house, so I would sometimes go there at lunch just to see daddy. Gina was so mean to him, and I just wanted to make sure he was okay. He always made me feel somewhat loved when it was just the two of us, then she would always find a way to ruin it by telling me how fucked up of a person I was.

That day I was talking to daddy about wrestling, because he always ordered the pay-per-view matches for Rome. Rome loved wrestling. While we were talking, Gina came and told me that Ronnie had been calling for me almost every day. I didn't want to talk to her at all. After all the bullshit I had dealt with in Atlanta, I didn't even want to hear what she had to say. I had enough issues to deal with, and I did not need that to come creeping back into my life, so I never called her back. I mean, what could she possibly have wanted? She had apologized, and I accepted. We hadn't seen each other since, so there was nothing to discuss.

Gina kept asking why I didn't want to talk to her. Then, she began to play a guessing game about what I had done to Rhonda to mess up the relationship. Once again, I supposedly damaged another relationship. I just ignored her and kept talking to daddy. I made an excuse to leave and told daddy I would be back to watch wrestling with him and Rome. I left running as usual, trying to get away from Gina. I was really getting sick of her ways, and the older I got, the more I wanted to call her out on her shit. I always managed to stop myself short of cussing her ass out, because she was my mother. I dreaded going home, and I no longer had a place of my own because Jessica moved out once the free rent was up, causing me to break the lease. Therefore, I was stuck with Rudy. All he did was go to work, drink with his buddies, cheat on me, fuck me, and then beat me. That was the cycle. I had no one to turn to, so I just tried to make my chaotic life as normal as possible. I was willing to take the abuse, but I didn't know how long it would or could last.

One day while at the mall, I ran into none other than Gene. I hadn't seen him in forever, and I was delighted to see his face. He seemed so happy to see me, but I could tell by his expression that he was shocked by the way I looked. I was a mess. I didn't care about my appearance, and the abuse had taken a toll on me. I wasn't eating, and my small frame was even smaller because I had lost about ten pounds. He hugged me, grabbed my hand, and pulled me to the nearest bench. I broke down crying on his shoulder and telling him all the issues I was having. He just held me and listened. He invited me back to his place. He was still at the spot where I attempted suicide, so it felt weird being in there. He begged me to eat his left over Chinese food, but I refused. He expressed that he was doing well, and he almost completely out of the drug game. He was even moving to North Carolina to better himself and sever all ties from his daunting past. I smiled, but I was hurt inside.

Ironically, after all the things he put me through, he was no longer seeing Kia. She had moved on for real, and he was moving down south. He was finally doing all the things I always wanted to do with him but he wasn't ready. He was living this privileged life while I was suffering with Rudy. That was fucked up. He kept hugging me and kissing me, and after multiple attempts of trying to have sex with me, I just let him do it. I don't even remember if it was good or not. I did my usual zone out thing. I laid there hoping for some type of love and affection, but instead I got nothing as usual. He kept saying that I needed to get myself together. It pissed me off that everyone always blamed me for my life. I was the victim here. I got dressed, and he kissed me goodbye and didn't even walk me to the door. It was weird and awkward. I didn't want to be with Gene, but he was still my husband legally and he had just basically screwed me with no sense of attachment or concern for me at all. I drove home feeling emptier than I had when I arrived at Gene's place.

When I got home, Rudy was there waiting for me.

"I've been trying to call you. Your mom and brother kept calling here for you. They said it was important, but they didn't say what they wanted."

I called Gina's house, but no one answered, so I decided to go over there. I asked Rudy to drive me, but he said he was tired and kept sitting on the couch. I rushed over thinking it was about daddy or Rome. When I got there Gina was half passed out, and Jerome was there picking up Rome. I hadn't seen him in a longtime. I just held my head down as he walked past me with Rome, so we wouldn't make eye contact. Mark was crying, and his wife was rubbing his back. Daddy was at the kitchen table with his head on the table. It had not felt like this in the house since Tim died.

"What's wrong with y'all? Who died?"

Everyone turned and looked at me. Daddy summoned me to the kitchen, and I joined him and just stood over his shoulder. Gina began to weep louder and louder. Finally, Daddy whispered that Ronnie was murdered in Atlanta. I fell to the floor and started crying but very silently so I would not overshadow Gina. My thoughts began to race and I wondered, *what happened? Who would kill my brother - well my sister, and why?* Even though we had it out after what happened, I still loved him.

Gina began screaming, "I told him to stop being a faggott! I knew it was going to get him killed."

I had no idea what she was talking about, so I just listened to her scream as I pieced the story together. Apparently it was all over the news in Atlanta. He was killed in a murder suicide by one of his roommates. Mark came into the kitchen to console me, and he hugged me and told me everything. One of Ronnie's roommates had recently found out that he was HIV positive when he went into some sort of rant and killed Ronnie and the other roommate. Then he killed himself after a ten-hour police standoff. I could see Mark's mouth moving, but I could not comprehend what he was telling me.

"Who was the killer?" I managed to ask.

Mark explained that the killer was the black one which would have to be Chuck. It took me a few minutes to process what he was telling me, because I knew I had slept with Chuck with no protection. I ran out of the house screaming, but it wasn't because of my brother's death. I was screaming because if Chuck was HIV positive, there was a strong chance that I was, too. There was no way I could fight having HIV because there was no cure for it. My life was truly over, and I was going to die. Mark and his wife came outside to get me, and basically carried me inside the house.

Gina immediately started yelling, "I lost two sons and you're screaming! They were my sons!"

I looked at her with the wrath of a little girl scorned. I wanted to kill her, because she was the evilest bitch I knew. Little did she know, Ronnie was dead, and I was next, but I was going to die a slow death. I couldn't tell them what happened in Atlanta. I just cried until I couldn't cry anymore. I wanted to die at times, but I didn't want to die from a disease like HIV. I wondered why Ronnie was calling so much and what he was trying to tell me. Guilt began to set in as I thought about the possibilities. Maybe I could have saved him. Maybe I could have helped him. I called to tell Rudy what was going on, and he just said sorry and that he was half sleep. He was such a bastard. I wanted to call Gene, but I knew he wouldn't come over with Mark being there. I just told Gina that Rudy was at work even though I knew he was on vacation for the next two weeks. I made my way to my old room and buried my head in the pillow.

My mind drifted to the day that Gina killed all my stuffed animals, the time Tim raped me, my first abortion, giving birth to Rome, being raped by Mike, and to my current abusive situation. I needed love from someone, and I needed it immediately. I decided to call Jerome. I knew he hated me, and he was married, but I also knew he had been there for me on multiple occasions. He answered and I immediately let all my pain out on him. I couldn't even get my words together.

"Brea, I'm coming to get you," he said as he came to my rescue like so many times in the past.

I hung up the phone and wiped my nose on my shirt. I didn't care about anything in that moment. I don't know what I was expecting from Jerome at that point. I just needed someone to give me love right at that very moment. I went outside to meet him. He pulled up, and he could barely stop before I was jumping into his car. I grabbed him and hugged him, and when I turned around, I could see Gina looking out the screen door.

"Pull off! Hurry!" I yelled.

Jerome sped off just as I asked, and we stopped at an empty parking lot a few streets over. I began to cry, and he held me so tight. I could see a few tears drop out of his eyes before he wiped them away. I told him a watered down story of the abuse that I was getting at the hands of Rudy. I could see the frustration in his eyes, and it was like he wanted more for me than I wanted for myself. He finally spoke.

"Brea, you need to leave all of these men alone, including me, and just get yourself together."

I hated that "get yourself together phrase." If I knew how, don't they think I would have by now? I continued to cry and he looked me in the eye and kissed me with the longest, deepest passionate kiss. I knew he still loved me even though I had hurt him. He told me he loved me and wanted the best for me, but he couldn't be with me because his wife didn't deserve that. I understood, and I really didn't want him anyway. I was just looking for some love, and he was usually there to love me or at least make me feel loved.

He took me back to Gina's after letting me cry on his shoulder for hours. I hugged him goodbye, and he told me to call him if I needed anything. I walked into Gina's house and daddy was asleep in the recliner while Gina was up looking at old photos. I told her that I was going home, and in a very odd way, she asked me to stay. So, we just sat there in silence looking at old photos before she went to sleep. I covered her up with the throw she had on the back of the couch, kissed daddy on the cheek, and headed home. Rudy was not there when I got there,

and I truly didn't care at all. I took a warm shower
and thought about my future or lack thereof. I was
going to die. I had to have HIV, and Chuck gave it to
me, and Savion or Ronnie had to give it to him, and
that's why he killed them. I was so fucked up, but I
knew I had to get up for work the next morning.
Rudy came in with the sun and just rolled over to
fuck me, and then went back to sleep. For a split
second, I wished I was HIV positive so Rudy would
have it, too. I hated him at this point.

For the next few days, I just went to work and
came home. I didn't really have the nerve to be
around my family or anyone for that matter. Gina
was planning Ronnie's funeral, and I was planning
mine in my head. I put in a request to up my life
insurance at work to $100k from the original $10k
that I had opted in for free. I never thought of dying
until now. The day came for us to bury Ronnie, and
Gina made sure he was buried as Ronnie. This
fucking bitch had him in a fucking three-piece suit, a
buzz cut, and some wing tip shoes looking like
Easter Sunday. I knew she, Rhonda, would have
wanted some six-inch heels, a nice little black dress,
and her weave laid, but that wasn't going to happen
on Gina's watch. Her son was born a man, and he
would die a man even though we all knew he was a
woman. I don't know what made me sadder, the fact
that my brother had died at the hands of another or
that the world, including his own mother, wouldn't
let him be himself even in his death.

The funeral was awful just as I expected. I
hadn't seen Ronnie since I drove out of the driveway.
I never thought that would be the last time I saw him
alive. I was so mad that day when I left Atlanta. After

the funeral, I heard Gina telling daddy that it was confirmed that Ronnie was HIV positive. She kept saying that it was because he was gay, but that was nonsense because Chuck wasn't gay and neither was I. Hell and if they had it, I did, too. Gina didn't know shit about HIV/AIDS or being gay or life period. She lived inside her head and believed everything she saw on TV. Rudy, of course, didn't go to the wake with me because he had to work. I hadn't heard from Gene besides a brief "I'm sorry." Jerome was there with his wife, so he barely said two words to me. All I could think about was my life being over. I was so scared about dying that way.

After everyone left, Jerome hung around to stay with Rome. His wife and parents had left. Gina was passed out drunk, and Mark went home with his family. Daddy was passed out in the basement, and I was left alone with Jerome after Rome passed out in his room. I grabbed his hand and pulled him into my old bedroom and began kissing him. I wanted him to make love to me since that's the way men showed love. I needed to have his love. All I had to do was seduce him like when we were kids, and that's just what I did. I pulled his pants down slowly while kissing his neck, and just that fast we were fucking because making love was just a figment of my imagination. In my heart, I knew I shouldn't be having sex with a married man without a condom, especially after finding out that I was probably HIV positive, but I didn't give a fuck. I was really only thinking about myself and my feelings. He came so fast that I didn't even realized he came inside of me. I mean, he always did, so that was nothing new. Jerome was so predictable.

He sat up on the edge of the bed with his face in his hand. He looked pissed. I walked over to kiss him, but he stopped me and told me he had to go, and he rushed out the door. I just let him go. I got what I wanted. I didn't necessarily want the sex, but that quick feeling of euphoria to last me for a couple of hours until I went home to be with my devil of a man, Rudy. I left without showering. I didn't care that I had just fucked someone else, and I was hoping Rudy knew. I got home to an empty house. You would think he would at least call to make sure I was okay or that I got home safely, but he didn't. That nigga wasn't shit.

He got home sometime during the night. I faked being asleep, but he made sure to wake me up to fuck, and I just laid there like Ms. Celie on the *Color Purple* while he got his rocks off like Mister. It was the worse. He made sure to not pull out, which I often asked him to do. He always expressed not wanting another child, but he sure never wanted to pull out. He rolled over and went to sleep, and I rolled the opposite way and went to sleep as well. My life sucked, and I was going to die. I needed to make my life worthwhile before it ended, and I needed to do it fast. I really did not know anything about HIV or even if I had it, but I knew it was a strong possibility. I just needed some answers, and I had to put my big girl panties on and go get them.

Chapter 14 - Only White People are Bipolar

My life was very routine after finding out that I may be HIV positive. I went to my dead-end office job that Gina was so proud to say I had because I was making "good" money in her eyes. If $35,000 a year with benefits was a good job, then I needed great, because this shit was not for me at all. After work, I would go see Rome every now and then. I mainly went there so I could sneak and meet Jerome to fuck in the back of my truck. Then, I would go home to my horrible man and fuck him, and I occasionally got choked, punched, or kicked for not being everything he needed and or wanted. It was a disaster of a life, and I knew it. I added fuel to the fire by reaching out to Gene and playing the victim only so he could give me sex and money. At this point, I was fucking all three of them with no condom or birth control, and I was possibly HIV positive and really didn't care. I did have some concern for Jerome, but he was so fucking gullible our entire life that it was hard for me to feel sorry for him. Daddy would always say, people only do to you what you allow them to do. I guess daddy knew firsthand, because Gina treated him like shit, and he just accepted it.

Gina was crazier than ever. She was talking to herself and not keeping up with her hygiene, which was not like her. The house was in shambles, and she didn't even have Rome as much. He was staying more with Jerome and his wife or with Jerome's parents and even with me when Rudy was working. Rome really didn't like Rudy now, and it showed. One day when Rome was over, Rudy and I got into a huge fight, and he was in my face yelling while I was backed in a corner in the closet. Rome ran into the room trying to push Rudy off of me.

"I'm not gone hit your mom, little boy," Rudy said right before he punched me in the mouth.

Rome was so scared and tried to get to me, but Rudy just threw him out the room and locked the door. When I took Rome to his dad, he told me how he had been dreaming about killing Rudy. He was only ten and I had him in the worst environment ever, so it was best that he did stay with Jerome. Daddy was worried about Gina, and he could barely get her to eat. She was so dramatic, so I just brushed it off as drama. She had been full of it my entire life. It was hard keeping up with the lifestyle that I was living, and I was back to having anxiety attacks. I would feel extremely depressed for days, sometimes weeks, then I would be extremely up beat and not able to sleep for days at a time. I was extremely stressed and could barely function at work or in life period. I mostly locked myself in the room at Rudy's house and tried to stay out of his way. I had a little money saved, but it wasn't enough to get my own place. I had run through the little $10k that Vick paid me off with, and the job was not going to cover all the bills I had.

Gene was leaving for North Carolina in a few days, so I made my way over to see him before he left. I was not totally in love with Gene, but I was extremely sad that he was leaving. I was probably jealous because he was getting to live the life I always wanted to live with him. He didn't even ask me to go. We just had sex and little talking was done. He didn't even treat me like his wife. Before I left his place, I went into the ridiculous crying rage very similar to what Gina did. He just hugged me and told me take care and get myself together. He did give me $500, but that didn't do shit but piss me off. I left extremely angry. I was enraged. I literally wanted to kill him. I was screaming and crying and I drove away from his place. I had the radio on full blast. I remember hearing Mary J Blige's "My Life" playing. I began to scream with tears rolling down my face as I sung along with Mary.

"If you look at my life, and see what I see. You would see I'm so blue, crying every day. I don't know what to do or to say."

Tears flowed continuously, and I could not get my composure. I knew it was about to happen. I was about to have an anxiety attack. I began to sweat, and I could feel my chest tightening up. I managed to pull into a gas station and tried hard to get my thoughts together, but I couldn't. Some lady kept asking me was I okay, but I was hyperventilating and holding my chest. She called 9-1-1. By the time they arrived, the attack had died down. Everyone was looking at me. The EMS guy checked me out and recommended that I go to the hospital, but I declined. The cop told me to call someone because he wasn't going to let me drive alone. I called Gina and Daddy, and Daddy came to get me. The owner of the gas station agreed to let me leave my car there until the next day. The ride back to Gina's house felt like an eternity. Daddy was talking to me and holding my hand. I just cried silently. The cop had told daddy what he and others had witnessed and that he needed to get me some kind of help. I already had the pills that the doctor gave me, but they didn't work.

Daddy began to discuss Gina. He always said that she loved me. I still felt like it was bullshit and wondered why he was bringing her up when no one was talking about her. He went on to explain that Gina had a very hard life growing up and that he didn't want me to end up old and miserable like her. I wasn't old yet, but I sure as hell was miserable. Daddy explained that Gina was sick and pointed to his head as he said sick. It was like he was trying to make me guess.

"Sick how, Daddy?"

He would not look at me, but he did say she had bipolar disorder. I just sucked my teeth, because I felt like only white people were bipolar. He explained that she was diagnosed as a child, but he did not know until a few years after he met her when she was hospitalized for it for weeks. Because of her bipolar, she could not function in society which is why she could never hold a job. I was actually relieved to hear that there was a name for it. That would explain all her manic and depressive behavior, but I still didn't believe she was sick like that. If so, why wasn't she in a crazy house? Daddy always made excuses for her. He told me that she never was good at taking her medicine, but she hadn't been talking it at all since Ronnie died and that she was drinking which intensified her condition. Why was daddy telling me this after all these years? Was I supposed to feel sorry for her? If I was, I didn't.

Daddy expressed his concern for me, because he saw the same behavior in me that he had seen in Gina when she was young. I knew I wasn't bipolar, because I wasn't crazy like her. I just acted like I did because of all the stuff that happened to me, but I was not a nut job like Gina. When we got to the house, Daddy asked me not to say anything about our conversation, and I promised I wouldn't - not that day anyway. I just wanted to rest. I left a message for Rudy explaining what happened and that I was going to stay the night at Gina's. His phone always went straight to voicemail. I never knew if he was working or whoring. I truly didn't care either way. I wanted out but didn't know how I was going to leave him just yet.

Gina was passed out on the couch when we walked in, and Rome was with his other grandparents. I was thinking about what Daddy had told me about Gina and even about Gene leaving for North Carolina, and I wished I had a fresh start. I knew I needed to see a doctor about possibly being HIV positive. I also needed to see a doctor about my mental state, especially since Daddy told me Gina was bipolar. I would only hope that shit wasn't hereditary, but somewhere deep inside I knew I was like her and it was scary.

I took a few days off from work to try to get myself together. I had been in the bed at Gina's house for a few days, and Rudy never thought one time to check on me. I finally decided it was time to go home, even though I really didn't want to go there. Nothing had changed in those few days that I was gone. That house was still so depressing. It looked like he had a wild party while I was gone. Rudy was very neat and clean, yet there were beer bottles all over. He left food on the stove and clothes scattered around the house. I just went upstairs looked at myself in the mirror for about fifteen minutes. My eyes were puffy, my hair my scraggily, and the cut under my eye was visible. What struck me as odd was that no one really asked what happened. It was like they knew but didn't want to ask, and I definitely wasn't going to volunteer. Even nosey Gina didn't ask what had happened to my eye. I wasn't even trying to hide it from her, so I know for a fact she saw it.

I needed to make some serious changes in my life, and the first thing I needed to do was find out if I was HIV positive. I looked in a phone book and found a place that did free HIV testing. I called and made an appointment under an alias name. I had to take the test the very next day, because I was due to go back to work the day after that. Rudy never even came home that night, and I was delighted. I didn't feel like fighting, and I sure as hell didn't feel like fucking. If I never fucked him again, that would be too soon.

That next morning, I got up, took a shower, pulled my long jet black hair back into a ponytail, and dressed in all black like I was headed to a funeral. Technically, I was going to find out if I was going to die, so I thought black fit the occasion. I threw on my black Versace shades that I borrowed from Tia many years ago, and I was ready to learn my fate. I pulled up to a building that was really a house that had been turned into an office for a nonprofit organization. I parked my car so far away that I probably walked a mile just to ensure no one would see me walk into the building. I slowly entered, and the receptionist was the loudest, most ghetto person I had ever encountered in my life.

"You here to get you a HIV test?" she asked while smacking a big piece of hot pink gum.

I was ready to smack that bitch.

I proceeded to the window and whispered, "I have an appointment. My name is Lisa Hoover."

She cracked a smile but really wanted to laugh, because there were not many people from my area with the last name of Hoover. Then, she asked me for ID. I was so confused as to why she needed ID. Like, just tell me if I have HIV and when I am going to die. I told her I didn't have ID, and the bitch got louder.

"You need ID to get a HIV test, because we have to report all positive tests to the state. You can't just be walking around HIV positive."

If I could have reached through that bullet proof glass, I would have beat her ass that day. I was not about to give her my ID. I felt my chest getting tight, and I knew I needed to get out of there. As I was leaving, I picked up all the pamphlets that were by the door, and one in particular stood out to me. It read:

"Having mood swings or feelings of Euphoria? Do you find yourself speaking extremely quickly for long periods of time? Do you have racing thoughts or rapid speech? If you answered yes to one or more of these questions, we can help."

It listed a toll-free number to call for help. The pamphlet also listed all the symptoms that I had always felt my entire life. On the front it had in big words: BIPOLAR DISORDER. I hurried out the door while the receptionist was yelling for me to reschedule. I just ignored her and rushed to the truck that was parked damn near in the next town.

When I finally made it to the truck, I threw all the pamphlets in the backseat, took my shades off, and began to pray and practice breathing to stop the attack that I was about to have. After a good ten to fifteen minutes of deep breathing and talking to myself, I finally calmed down enough to drive myself home. I was sweating so bad that I had taken my shirt off, and I was down to my bra. I still was no closer to knowing if I was HIV positive than I was when I left the house that morning. I got home to Rudy screaming at me for leaving the porch light on and for not having anything cooked for dinner. I was wondering what the fuck he did before he met me and for the few days that I was at Gina's. He was foaming out the mouth and yelling, but I remained calm. He grabbed me by my hair and dragged me around the house showing me all the things that needed to be done. I pulled his hands off of my hair and made it upstairs.

I sat on the edge of the bed while he was downstairs screaming about everything. I reached into my purse for the pamphlet that I took from the clinic. I reviewed the list of resources that was printed on the back. I waited until he fell asleep and called the hotline. The lady asked me a lot of personal questions and a lot about my family history, especially about my mother and father. I did mention to her that Gina may be bipolar, but I wasn't sure. Based on my family history and the symptoms that I had been having, she recommended a doctor for me to visit. For the next few days, I just tried to stay away from Rudy, but I needed a plan to get away from him. The time had come for me to go see the doctor. I definitely needed some kind of help, because my mind was all over the place.

The doctor was very old, and I wasn't expecting that. He asked me about all the issues I was having. I broke down crying and explained everything to him. I told him how I had anxiety my whole life and how I tried to kill myself. I told him about me being raped, and I even told him that I may have HIV. I knew he wouldn't tell anyone, and I just needed to get it off my chest. I didn't tell him the specific details, but I did lay it on the line for him. He was convinced that I had more than depression. He was concerned, and he did say that I had several signs of bipolar disorder. He scheduled a cat scan of the brain and some other tests for me. He also gave me a note to be off work for two weeks until he could make a clear diagnosis. I thought to myself, *bipolar? Did that mean I was going to have to live in a crazy house?* I didn't know anything about it.

He wanted me to bring Gina in with me for my next appointment. I didn't how I was going to do that, because Gina didn't like folks in her business. I didn't know anything about Gina besides the fact that she was crazy. I decided to ask her anyway. I told her how I was feeling and that I needed her to go with me. She agreed, but she wasn't happy about it. Just her agreeing was odd to me, because she hated me, and she was a bitch about everything. Gina was still acting unlike herself, and she had very erratic behavior. Like, she had the most beautiful hair down her back, and she abruptly cut it all off. This was odd for her, because she bragged about her hair and skin color all the time. To my surprise, she kept her word and decided to go to the shrink with me. Of

course she had her dark shades on - we both did.
Gina had made me paranoid about what other people
thought of me. We went back to see the old man.

"Dr. Roth, I thought you were dead," Gina said
as she leaned in to hug him.

How did she know him, and why would she
hug him? He was extremely happy to see her and
immediately asked her if she was taking her
medication. She began to look uncomfortable, and I
knew it was because I was there. I just stared with a
look of confusion on my face. Gina suddenly broke
down crying.

"Gina, calm down and tell your daughter a
little bit about yourself. She needs help, and I'm
going to help her like I helped you."

Why was he talking to her like that, and why
was she so vulnerable? It was like she was a different
person around him. We had only been in the room
for five minutes and Gina had turned into a person I
had never seen before, and it made me nervous. He
proceeded to coach her into telling me about her life.
She started out talking about her childhood, but she
being extremely evasive. He sat next to her and held
her hand as she laid on his shoulder and closed her
eyes. I sat on the edge of my chair with such
suspense, because Gina had never talked about her
life. She began to tell me her story.

Apparently, her life was fucked up from birth.
She was born to an Irish mother and a black father.
Her mother was sixteen and was forced to give Gina
away, because even though she was half white when
she was born you could tell she was black, and
Gina's mother's parents were extremely prejudice.
So, she was raised by her father's mother who hated

light-skinned black folks and made it known to Gina every chance she got.

Gina's father was married to a woman who also hated light-skinned people, and all of his other children had a complexion darker than Gina's. She was forced to sleep in the outside shed with no heat in the winter, and they made it clear that they didn't want her around. When she was twelve, she was gang raped by four local boys, and her half-sister just sat there, watched, and taunted her while the gang raped her. That's why she hated Draya's mom, because of what happen to her as a child. She told her grandmother about the rape, but she blamed Gina for being loose. Gina was telling me this story while being consoled by the doctor, and for the first time in my life I believed her. She was not lying or being manipulative. She then began to explain how she finally escaped the abusive environment. She then married a great man and had three kids by him, but he was tragically killed in a bar fight. Gina was left to raise the three boys alone until she married her second husband who was abusive. He molested the boys on more than one occasion.

I sat back in my seat and just watched my mother who had been so mean and so cruel to me my entire life. I watched her have a soul and a heart, but she was fucked up just like me. I did feel sorry for her, but I also was mad, because if she went through all of this, why didn't she protect me? Why didn't she love me? What had I done to her? Gina was in a daze, and it was like it wasn't her as an adult anymore. It appeared that she went into a childlike demeanor, and the doctor began to rub her back and talk to her as if she were a child. I had never seen anything like that, and I was very frightened by it. She actually fell asleep and he carried her to lie on the sofa. He motioned for me to come with him. He took me to another room and began to explain that Gina had come to him for help after she left her second husband, and she was in bad shape very similar to the way I was a few days prior. He explained that Gina was beyond bipolar, and that she also had bouts of split personality trait. This all was overwhelming and way over my head.

He explained that my daddy had called him, and they were trying to come up with a plan to get her some long term treatment, but she would never agree to it. After seeing what shape she was in, she was going to need it and fast. He explained to me that based on my testing, my symptoms, and my family history, I was for sure bipolar. He also told me that he could help me, but I had to take the medication. He said that with his help I could possibly be off them in a short period of time with intense therapy. This was all too much for me to take in at once. Gina had been through hell and back, and that's why she was so fucked up and now I was bipolar.

I remember seeing stuff like this on TV, but I didn't know black people could get it. The doctor went on and explained how people live and function with bipolar, and if I really listened to him he could help me. However, he seemed extremely concerned about Gina, and he told me that I heard the watered down story of her life. He did say, which I knew he wasn't supposed to, that Gina was gang raped so bad that she was hospitalized for it, and that not only did her sister watch, but she also participated. It made sense why Gina hated her family and why Daddy would not let me go over there.

I took the script from the doctor, and we walked back so I could get Gina. She was still sleep, He gently woke her up and gave her a prescription as well and made us both an appointment to follow up with him in one week. She was still in a daze, so I grabbed her hand, and she laid on my shoulder as we walked out the door. I helped her get into the truck. I got in and she just put her shades on, and we didn't say a word to each other on the twenty-minute drive back home. We just sat in silence. For the first time in life, I saw Gina as a person, even if it was only for a few hours. I wasn't the only one fucked up. I was so fucked up, because my mother was fucked up. On top of everything I had been dealing with, the doctor said I was bipolar. We both looked at each other when we got home.

Gina paused, and then said, "Brea, don't be telling nobody my business, girl. That was a long time ago. Let's just leave it there."

I nodded my head in agreement and helped her to the house. I didn't even go in, because I didn't want to see daddy. I drove in silence wondering how I was going to handle all these trials and why did God pick me to deal with them. It was all too much for one person to handle, and I knew I would have to do it alone, but I was not ready.

Chapter 15 - Shelter Life

After being diagnosed with bipolar, I got even more depressed. I filled the prescription, but I did not want to take the medication. I was due to go back to work, and I just lied and told the doctor that I was taking my medication so he would release me. Gina didn't go back to see him, which I knew she wouldn't. When I would go over to see Rome, she was just there laid out on the couch in her house gown. I tiptoed around the house trying not to bother Rudy. We just kept up with our usual routine. He would go out, work, party, and then come home to fuck and fight on me. I was used to it. I had started back to work, and I was going to be as normal as I possibly could. I was still feeling extremely depressed, but I managed to call the folks on the phone and harass them about the money they owed my company, and I did the job great. I would always get a good bonus pay. I was trying to save up, because I really wanted to leave Rudy bad.

I had been feeling lonely and decided to call Jerome to meet me. He did of course, and we did our usual sex in the truck, but I wanted to talk also. I cried and told him that I wanted to leave Rudy and be with him. I know he wanted to be with me, but I didn't want to be with him. I just wanted attention. He just hugged me and said someday we would be together. It pissed me off, even though I knew I didn't want to be with him at all. I just said okay, and we parted ways. I just liked to be with Jerome because I controlled him, and it made me feel good since Rudy controlled my life. I reached out to Gene as well, and he had not left yet, even though he said he was leaving a few weeks ago. I began to wonder if he was really going or just saying that. I quickly went to his place to get a second dose of loving from him as well. I loved being with him, because he was passionate and the sex was always very intense. However, the feelings were lost, so it wasn't quite the same. His place was all packed, and he did tell me that would be the last time he saw me for a while. We didn't talk divorce or reconciliation, we just fucked and I left.

I was dreading going home to Rudy, and I didn't want to go to Gina's. I had a really weird feeling, but I went home anyway. I just wanted to go home, take a shower, and not fight or fuck Rudy. He was home on the couch as usual. I ran upstairs to take a shower, and he came up starting with me. It was like he wanted to fight. I got out the shower, and he took my towel off of me. I went to get another towel, and he told me not to, because all the towels were his. I proceeded to the bedroom wet and naked, and I started drying off with one of my t-shirts. He just stood there taunting me.

"Look at you. You're a mess and don't no man want you but me, so you need to treat me better."

I just started laughing, because I knew I had just fucked two men, and I could fuck a whole lot more. My laughing pissed him off, but I didn't give a fuck. I managed to get my panties and bra on before he jumped on me and started choking me. He was on top of me on the bed choking me out. I was moving my hands, but he was so big that he was going to kill me. I was grabbing everything that I could from the night stand, and I managed to get my hands on an ink pen. I jabbed him in his neck with it as hard as I could. He let me go, and I was gasping for air. A few more seconds of being choked, and I would have been dead. There was a set of weights next to the bed. I immediately picked up the 10lb weight, and threw it at him. It landed on his foot. I jumped on him and started punching, biting, kicking, and doing anything I could to him.

He was holding his foot and screaming, "Bitch, you broke my foot!"

I ran out the door past him. Wearing just my panties and bra, I ran up and down the street screaming.

"Help! Help! Call the cops now! Hurry!"

Just then, I saw a lady, and she let me in her car and called 9-1-1. The police came out, and I knew one of the guys. I told them everything that happened, and I had the bruises to prove it. They drove me back around to the house and gave me a jacket to put on since I was practically naked. The best feeling was seeing Rudy escorted out the house in cuffs and put in a cop car by his buddy. I ran in the house to get as much of my belongings as I possibly could.

They took me down to the station to file a report. I don't know why I called Gina looking for sympathy, but she made it clear that I could not stay there anymore.

"Brea, you should have just listened. Rudy is a good man, and he got a good job. Now he gone lose it because of you."

I just hung up. Then, the cops advised me that I could go to a domestic violence shelter. I remembered when I tried to go before and he stopped me. I was excited to go. I remembered the lady saying how much they could help me, so I went with excitement. I was able to get dressed while I was at the police station. They took me back to get my car, and I loaded what I could into it. I then proceeded to follow the cops to an empty lot where I was met by a middle aged white woman who looked like a nun. I followed her on a long path back to a building that looked like an old school. We went into the building and went to the main office. We sat down, and she had a stack of papers for me to fill out. She asked me about how many children I had and if I wanted to get a restraining order, which I for sure did. I knew if I ever saw Rudy again, he would kill me.

She went over the house rules and advised me that I would be sharing a room since I was alone. I never shared a room with another female, and I really didn't get along with other people, but I was determined to make this work. She told me they could help me with housing and getting custody, or at least shared custody, of Rome. She told me the average person stayed for sixty days, but they had a ninety days maximum. She also asked if I had been exposed to the HIV virus, and I quickly said no. I was not about to mess this up by bringing up that HIV thing. She showed me the kitchen, and they had loads of food in the pantry.

There was a group of women and children in the living room area. They introduced themselves to me and I did the same. She then showed me the laundry area and finally to my room. She took out a key ring with a bunch of keys on it. It reminded me of when I was in elementary school and the janitor would be walking by with all those keys. It was a room with a bunk bed and a twin bed, two dressers, and a personal bathroom. I would be in there alone for now, but she did tell me a lady with a two year old would be coming in the morning. She gave me some sheets and told me that everyone would be going to bed soon, and she told me the curfew. I was just happy to be away from Rudy. Anything was better than being with him. I made my bed and laid down for a good night's sleep.

That next morning, I woke up to the smell of bacon. It was a Saturday morning, and I still didn't have a roommate. They had a phone in the common area that we could use as long as we didn't stay on it too long. I called to talk to Rome, but he was with Jerome. I decided to call Jerome and tell him what was going on with me. He sounded relieved that I was safe. I told him that I was going to get my life together and that they were going to help me. I also expressed wanting to get Rome on a full-time basis, and he was on board with that, too. I told him that I would not be having sex with him or anyone else for that matter, because I needed to get myself together, and he totally understood. I hung up feeling pretty good. I walked into the kitchen and a young white girl was in there cooking.

"Want some breakfast?" she asked.

I surely was hungry. I sat down and ate the bacon, eggs, and pancakes that she had prepared. She was trying to talk to me, but I was not trying to make friends at all. I ate quickly and went back to my room. I had brought my radio in, so I could play my cd on it. My cell phone was blowing up, and I knew it was Rudy calling, so I didn't even check it. They really wanted us to use the common phone because a lot of the woman would go back to their abuser and never finish the program, but that would not be me. I was going to use everything they gave me. I heard a knock at the door, and it was another lady with a young girl. She was probably about nineteen with the cutest little girl who was about two. She introduced her baby to me and told me that she would be my new roommate. I said hello, and she began to put her stuff on the bunkbed and then just sat there looking lost. I made small talk and told her I had a ten year old son, and she warmed up a little bit. By the time she relaxed, it was time to attend a group meeting. This was where all the women met up daily for a therapy session.

The discussion that day was self-love. She asked everyone what was self-love and how did we begin to have self-love and how did we get to know our worth. Everyone was quiet, but she didn't force us to talk. She offered for us to share our stories, and some women did, but I sure as hell wasn't about to tell these strangers all my business. One lady shared a story about her twenty year marriage and how she finally left. Her husband had her locked in the basement and fed her like a dog.

Another girl was sharing that she had broken ribs and showed us where she had a missing back tooth. There were other people in this world besides me who had crazy stories. I was not alone. I had always felt so alone my entire life, and for the first time, I didn't. I listened to everything the lady said about loving yourself first, and she said it's okay to be alone. She explained how happiness starts from within. I always thought I had to get happiness from someone else. She told us to look in the mirror every day and say, *"You are beautiful. You are worthy to be happy."* I thought she was crazy. I was not about to look in the mirror and talk to myself. I did that enough. The meeting was okay. Afterwards, I went back to my room. There was no one without kids there with them, so it felt very odd being there alone, but I just stayed to myself.

For the next couple of weeks, I just worked and came back to the shelter. I took in all the information that they were telling and tried my best to apply it to my life. I did not answer any of Rudy's calls, but I did listen to all his many voicemails which were all crazy. One minute he loved me and wanted to make it work, then the next minute he was cussing at me, because he was suspended without pay. He also said I had fractured his foot with the weight I threw at him. That made me smile. I was hurting him the way he hurt me. I didn't feel sorry for his ass. Our relationship was only a few months long, and he had put me through so much hell in that short period of time. I had not been feeling well at all and had been extremely tired. I was also very sick. I felt like I was pregnant, but I was not late on my period. I was paranoid and bought a test from the local drug store, but it came out negative. Thank God because, who knows who would have been the daddy.

The lady at the shelter was helping me find a place, and they were going to pay two months of rent for me, which would give me a good push. I found a two bedroom apartment in a pretty decent area, and I could move within the next two weeks. I was so happy to finally have something that was mine. I had even started doing some of the girls' hair at the shelter. They assured me that they would come to me after I left, so I would have extra income from

doing hair and my job. I was going to get my salon. I
had a plan to save all the money I got from doing
hair and pay bills with the money from my job. I was
going to court for my restraining order against Rudy.
The social worker from the shelter was supposed to
come with me, but at the last minute she could not
go. I saw Rudy as soon as I walked in the building.
This nigga had a nerve to sit right next to me. He
grabbed my hand and kissed it and told me he really
wanted me back and that he was seeing a counselor
about his anger. He even complimented me on how
good I looked. Since I had been in the shelter, I was
taking good care of myself again.

I was trying my best not to look at him, but I
couldn't help but feel a little bad. I did cause him to
lose his job, and he seemed so genuine, but I was not
going to listen to him. When we got in the courtroom,
the judge began to ask me questions, and all I could
think about was if I moved forward, he would lose
his job and not be able to take care of his son. I lied
to the judge and told him I didn't feel threatened by
him and that I did not want to proceed with the
restraining order. Rudy was crying and thanking me,
and the judge dismissed the case. I wasn't strong
enough to do that to him. His job and his child were
his life, but I was still not going to go back to him. I
hurried to the car trying to avoid him, but of course
he was on my heels.

"Brea, I love you," he slowly whispered in my
ear. "Thank you so much. Please come home."

I looked him in the eye and just hopped in the
truck with him standing there looking at me like I
was crazy. On the long ride back to the shelter, I just
kept thinking that I had made a huge mistake and

that I really should have taken the advice of the social worker. I had let him get inside my head. I still did not love myself enough to know any better. I arrived back at the shelter and everyone asked me how it went. I lied and told them that I got the restraining order. They were so happy and clapping, and the white girl who loved to cook even made a cake that night to celebrate. I felt so bad about not getting the restraining order and for lying to those people who really took a liking to me. I was having that anxious feeling and began to get extremely depressed.

The next day the social worker pulled me in the office and explained how she knew I did not file for the restraining order. I felt ashamed. She told me she was worried because she knew men like Rudy, and they didn't let go easily. I had shared majority of the truth with her. I told her I was not going back and that when I moved he would not know. I mean we didn't have any children together, so I didn't have to see him. Plus, I was moving to a different county, so I would probably never run into him, at least I hoped I wouldn't. She said some very critical words that stuck with me.

"Brea, I pray you don't regret this, and I pray you don't lose your life."

I just brushed her off and went back to my regular routine. I was preparing to move to my new apartment, and I was so excited. When I was leaving the shelter, they gave me a microwave and a new set of dishes, and they were even having a bedroom set delivered to the new house. Gina, Rome, and Daddy were going to meet me there. I exchanged numbers with my roommate. She had also found a place, and I knew we would be staying in touch. I had been there for sixty-six days, and my time had come to an end. The truck was loaded with all kinds of goodies, and I was on my way. I arrived at my apartment and Rome and Daddy were waiting at the door. Gina was in the car looking drunk. We walked in and Rome was so happy as he ran to his new room. It was empty but he was having his bedroom set delivered the next day.

"You like it, Daddy?" I asked feeling relieved.

"I love it, Brea. I'm so proud of you."

Gina went in, of course, "Brea, you got to keep this place clean. This is too nice of a place for you to fuck it up with your lazy triflin' ass."

I just ignored her, and all that sympathy I had for her previously went right out the window. Daddy bought us some hoagies from Carmen's, the best place in South Jersey. It was always packed, and the aroma was delightful. I was so stuffed that I ran to the bathroom and threw up. I attributed it to me eating like a pig, but Ms. Gina was reading into it much deeper.

"I hope your stupid ass ain't pregnant."

She always embarrassed me, especially in front of Rome. I quickly put that to rest.

"You have to have sex to get pregnant," I said with an attitude.

She just looked at me and rolled her eyes. Daddy knew it was time to get her out of there.

"Ok guys, let's go."

Rome begged to stay with me, and Gina finally agreed.

After they left, Rome and I laid around and watched DVDs all night. We fell asleep on the floor, and I remember him saying he loved me. I told him that I loved him too, but I said it real fast. I didn't know how to show him any real affection, but he was happy. Over the next few weeks, the apartment had been fully furnished, and I was going to work. I had still been feeling sick, and I started to know that something was wrong. I was too scared to take a pregnancy test because I didn't want to deal with that again. So I just ignored it like I had done everything else. I had a period, but it was only one day. However, I still had one so I couldn't be pregnant. Could I? I did have unprotected sex with three men, but I just attributed it to the change of weather. Rome had been staying over a lot, and Gina only agreed because I gave her a key so she could pop up as she pleased. She did that often, especially when Rome was there. She would just walk in without knocking.

One night Rome was asleep, and I was so alone. I did the unthinkable and called Rudy. He convinced me to talk, but I couldn't leave Rome to go meet him, and I didn't want to take Rome to Gina's that late. I knew she would be bitching. I felt extremely hesitant, but I told him where I lived so he could come over. After all the hard work I had done, I still let him back into my life. We were in the car talking at first. Then, he convinced me to let him come upstairs. He was very charming and had a way of convincing me to do things that I didn't want to do. I agreed to let him come up against my better judgement. I showed him around a little, and then took him to my room. He started kissing me, but I really didn't want to have sex with him. However, once again, he talked me into it, or more like seduced me into it. We had amazing sex that night, and it took me back to that euphoric feeling that I had. I woke up and the sun was up. I was shaking him to wake him up. He was not budging, and I did not want Rome to see him, because I knew he would tell Gina and maybe even his dad. I was trying to get closer to my son not further apart. He finally woke up, but with an attitude.

"Damn, Brea, you go ahead to work I'll stay here until you get back."

I was in deep trouble, because he was acting like we were together. Rome was up, and I could hear him playing the game. I came out to tell him to get dressed, but he already was, and he looked really sad. I got dressed, and Rome and I left for school and work, while leaving Rudy back at my apartment. As soon as we got in the truck, Rome started crying.

"Why did you bring him back to our house mom? I thought you were getting better."

He must have been listening to our conversation, because he did know what kind of car Rudy, but of course he knew Rudy's voice. I went into instant defense mode.

"Little boy, I'm the mom, and I do what the fuck I want. You better not tell Gina or your dad shit, or I'm going to give your game away. And, stop that fucking crying like a little bitch."

He sucked it up real fast and took the napkin out of his lunch bag to wipe his face. I could understand why he was pissed, but I didn't know what to say to him. I dropped him off and went to work. I was on edge all day and my heart was racing. I decided to leave early, because I had so much on my brain. I could not get my thoughts together. I hadn't been to see the doctor in a while because I was doing so well, but I could feel my heart jumping out my chest. I knew I had fucked up by letting Rudy come there.

When I got home, this nigga was still sleep. It was the middle of the day, and he needed to get up. He was still suspended for another incident with him and a female officer getting into a heated argument on the job. I woke him up and told him it was time to go because Gina was coming. I just said that. He did get up and put all his clothes on but not before fucking me one last time. It was not as good as it was that previous night. He kissed me and told me he would be back later. I didn't want him to come back, but I didn't know what to say or how to get rid of him.

I told Rome to stay at Gina's when he got out of school, and I know he thought it was because of Rudy. Well, it was because of Rudy, but not for the reasons he thought. I had been so tired and sick that I dozed off. I woke up to a loud bang on the door. It was Rudy. He had been calling me, but I was asleep and didn't hear my phone. I opened the door to a drunk and horny Rudy. I told him I didn't feel well and that I needed rest. He bombarded his way into the house looking in the closets and making a lot of noise. I kept asking him to be quiet because I had neighbors downstairs. He didn't care and seemed to get louder after I told him that. He was such an asshole. After all the hard work I had done to get rid of him, I was back where I started before I entered the shelter. My life sucked again that fast. What was I thinking? I wasn't thinking.

I managed to calm him down and get him in bed. He started getting on top of me and fell asleep before we could even start to have sex. I just laid there with my pants halfway pulled down and this 6'7" man on top of my 5'5" 119lb frame. I began to cry but very silently. All I could think of was the social working saying she hoped I wouldn't regret not getting a restraining order. I regretted a lot at that moment, especially not being strong enough to make a sound decision not to call Rudy. I wish I made better choices, but I didn't. I was right where I started a few months back, before entering the shelter. My life couldn't be any worse than it was at this moment, and it was all my fault.

Chapter 16 - Time to Take the Test

Rudy had been coming over more and more, and he practically lived there. I had been back to my shrink, and I finally filled the script for Lithium. I still wasn't feeling better, and I was tired all the time. The doctor said that the medication would do that to me. I had been paranoid about having HIV more and more. It seemed like everything symptom I had was a symptom of HIV. The more I saw the doctor, the more I wanted to be tested. He explained to me that just how I could live with bipolar, I could also live with HIV, but the key was to get tested. I was going to work still every day, but I was fucking up there. I was passed up on a promotion because I missed too much time, and I was pissed after that, so I wasn't really putting in much work. I had gained quite a few pounds, and I was feeling like I was pregnant. I hadn't had a period in a while, but I was so scared to take a test. More than likely I would be pregnant by Rudy, and that would be a disaster.

Rome didn't want to come over to stay with me at all, because everyone knew Rudy wasn't shit - even Gina. Although, she made it seem like he was God's gift to me. He was more like God's punishment to me. I was so scared to tell Rudy that I may be pregnant, because he always said he didn't want any more kids. He was back working because they threw out that case that was pending against him. He always managed to get away with everything. He wasn't living with me, but he was pretty close to it. He had clothes, sneakers, and even a work uniform at my house. We really hadn't fought much, but he did make me feel like less of a woman. He would always say I was fat. I did gain about ten pounds, but I wasn't even 130 pounds. He would also tell me that I was ugly and that I needed to do something with my hair. I didn't want to do anything with myself. He made me feel so low.

Gina would not bring Rome over while Rudy was there. Rome would always express his hate for Rudy. Rudy wasn't good enough to be around Rome, but he was good enough for me in Gina's eyes. How could she like a man that beat me? She had been in that situation before, so it seems she would understand. Then again we were talking about Gina here. I had scheduled an appointment at the gynecologist to get a pregnancy test and an HIV test. I was determined to do it. The day came for me to go take the test, and Rudy was at my place. He picked a fight with me and gave me a busted lip. There was no way that I was going to the appointment like that, so I just cancelled the appointment. I could easily buy a pregnancy test from the drug store, but I was so scared, and Rudy had been lingering around. I decided I would just suck it up and get the pregnancy test, because his ass wasn't leaving any time soon.

I made the trip to the drug store later that night while Rudy was asleep. I was prepared wearing my all black and my dark shades just as I had learned from Gina. I went straight to the right aisle and picked up the pregnancy test. As I walked by, I saw another test that read: *In-home HIV Test*. I couldn't believe they had a test for HIV just like they did for pregnancy. The only difference was that I had to use saliva for the HIV test. I slipped my glasses off and read the label, and right there before me was a test that I could take to find out if I was HIV positive without anyone knowing. This was too good to be true. The test was $50, and I didn't have enough cash on me. So, I just left both tests there and decided I would just go back to get them the next day. I went back home and couldn't sleep. I was happy that I could get the results of the HIV test without having to go inside the clinic, but I was still nervous because I didn't know how I would react if I had the disease. I finally fell asleep on the sofa, and Rudy made sure to wake me up as he left. I asked to talk to him for a few minutes.

"Rudy, I'm a little late getting my period, and I'm a little concerned that I may be pregnant."

He quickly dismissed me and told me that I was not pregnant. He said that I just wanted to be pregnant, so I needed to calm down. Then, he walked out the door. How could he be so sure? This nigga busted a nut inside me every chance he got, but he really felt like I *wanted to be pregnant*. I got up and got ready for work. On my way to the job, I stopped at that same drug store to pick up the two tests. I made sure I had my dark shades on, because I didn't need anyone seeing me with an HIV test in my hand. Of course on this day, the store was packed. I held the tests underneath my purse, trying to conceal them as much as I possibly could. When it was finally my turn, I quickly placed the tests on the counter. After waiting in the line and doing all that I could to be discreet, the cashier said very loudly, "You can't buy no HIV test up here. You gotta take that back to the pharmacy."

Why was that bitch so fucking loud? Everyone was staring at me like I was some sort of dope fiend.

I rushed back to the pharmacy and checked out. The sexy pharmacist did advise me that I would still need to be tested by a doctor, because I could get a false negative or positive results. If the test said negative, there was no way that I was taking that shit over. Oh hell no. I was going to accept those results. I rushed out and headed to work. I was going to get this tests done today right at work.

As soon as I got to work, I entered the first floor bathroom, but it was so crowded, and there was no privacy whatsoever. I knew there was a bathroom upstairs that I would frequent when I had to poop. It was more private, but someone was in there. I went back to my desk after twenty minutes of trying to get that done with no success. I left for the day feeling defeated. I hid the tests in my truck inside a pocketbook that I had never used. I stuffed it under all the junk I had in the back of my truck.

I went home to a meal cooked by Rudy. It seemed nice, but I knew it wouldn't last long. I couldn't eat much without feeling sick. He had made spaghetti, and the smell of the garlic in the red sauce was making me gag. I ran to the bathroom and threw up the remnants of the Cobb salad that I had for lunch. He ran in to see if I was okay. I just told him that ate some spoiled food earlier. I began to think I was pregnant more and more. We did our usual fuck and go to sleep, but I was grateful that I didn't have to fight that grown man that night. I just laid there wide awake thinking about the two tests and what the results would be. I promised God that I would not have a 5th abortion. However, I was not a good mom to Rome, so it would be stupid to bring another child into my dysfunctional chaos. Plus, I knew I would not be able to live with HIV, and just to think if I had it that meant I gave it to Jerome, Rudy, and even Gene. I didn't know how I would be able live with either positive result – let alone, both being positive. I just needed to do it and get it over with, so I could figure out what I would do next.

The next morning, I wore my usual all black. I was feeling extremely depressed, and I really didn't want to get out of bed. I knew this was my only chance to take the tests, because Rudy was off that day, and it was clear that he was not going home anytime soon. I ran to the truck without waking him and checked the purse in the backseat to ensure my tests were still there. I suddenly heard loud banging, and it was Rudy at my window. I quickly pushed the junk back on top of the purse and rolled down the window.

"You scared me, Rudy," I said wondering what he wanted.

He leaned in, gave me a kiss, and said "You didn't kiss me goodbye, and you seem a little upset. Is everything ok?"

I thought to myself, "*No dumb ass, everything is not okay. I'm probably pregnant by your abusive ass, and I'm probably HIV positive, which I would have gotten from my gay brother's lover. So, no I am not okay.* Instead of verbally responding, I just nodded yes, and he let me leave and watched me drive off.

It seemed like it took me forever to get to work. I did my work as fast as I could, and I was determined I would take the tests at lunch. I forgot we were having a birthday lunch for one of the girls, which would alter my plans a bit. I knew everyone used the upstairs bathroom more so after lunch to poop, so I just waited until close to the end of the day when everyone was gone to ensure I was all alone. I grabbed my bag and headed upstairs. I checked my purse and held it close to me like a scared white girl being followed by three black men. I entered the restroom which had about four stalls in it and looked to make sure it was empty. I went into the handicap stall to have more room.

So, there I was at that bullshit 9 to 5 where I was overworked and underpaid about to take these two tests. I knew how to take a pregnancy test, so I just peed on the stick and set the test on top of the toilet paper dispenser. Now with the HIV test, I would need to read the directions in detail. There was a long swab that looked like a long Q-tip. I was to swab my mouth and put it in the solution. If it changed colors, then I was HIV positive. I was to wait fifteen minutes for the HIV test results. I closed my eyes, swabbed my left check, and put it in the solution. I placed it next to the pregnancy test which I had upside down so I wouldn't see it. After about ten minutes of waiting, I heard someone come into the restroom. Damn it, I was so screwed. I just stayed quiet. Whoever it was made sure they blew it up, and I was gasping for air, but I just remained quiet. I knew that they would leave, and they did without even washing their hands.

I stood up and turned the pregnancy test over and picked up the HIV test. Shit, one positive and one negative. I didn't know how to feel. According to the tests, I was pregnant, and I did NOT have HIV. I was relieved and upset at the same time. I did promise God that I would never have another abortion, but I could not have a baby by abusive ass Rudy. I was extremely grateful that I didn't see any color in that tube. I was clear on that. It was well over three months since I had that encounter with Chuck. The test literature said that three months was the rule, but I should still retest with a professional. I was still relieved by those results. I stuffed all the trash and tests into my purse and made a quick exit. I logged out of my system and ran out the door. I made sure I pulled around the back at the job to put both tests in the big green garbage bin that was collected for all the units in the plaza. I didn't want any traces of those tests on me.

I headed home with extreme anxiety. I didn't want to tell Rudy that I was pregnant, because he made it clear he didn't want any kids. I had also slept with Gene and Jerome, and I really didn't know how far along I was. I had gained quite a few pounds and I had been having signs of pregnancy since I was in the shelter. I walked in the house to start dinner. I had been craving a steak so bad. I made a great salad and some baked potatoes. I was really trying to set the stage for Rudy so I could tell him, even though I was extremely nervous.

I thought maybe my being pregnant would change him. He was very good with his son, and he would have to love this baby just the same. Or, maybe I could just break this one little promise to God and get an abortion, even though I really didn't want to do it. Rudy came in late, and I was asleep. He woke me up to warm up his food. I did without complaining since I chose to let him enter back into my life. I brought up being pregnant again, but I didn't bring it up in a way to make him suspicious. I just told him we needed to protect ourselves so I wouldn't get pregnant.

He just laughed and replied, "Brea, I had a vasectomy five years ago. I knew I never wanted anymore children."

My mouth hit the floor, and I just swallowed really hard and shook my head to confirm that I understood. He came over and smacked me on the ass so hard.

"We can have all the unprotected sex we want, baby."

So this meant I was pregnant by Jerome, or even worse Gene. Holy shit! I hadn't even talked to Gene, and Jerome was married. This also meant I was at least 10-12 weeks, so I needed to get an abortion and fast.

Chapter 17 - Is He Dead?

I went on with life day by day. I was so afraid
of Rudy finding out I was pregnant. I began to fake
my period like every week and told him I had a yeast
infection, so he would not touch my stomach. I was
big, and I even think I felt a movement but I brushed
it off as gas. I finally was able to get enough money to
get the abortion, and I had my appointment that
Saturday. I was probably about twelve weeks, and I
needed to get it done because the clinic I went to
only did them up to fourteen weeks. Otherwise, I
would have to go to a clinic in Northern New Jersey
and do a two-day procedure. There was no way that I
could do that. I did the cab thing and paid someone
like I had done in the past. I arrived at the same
clinic for the fifth time. I should have been on a first
name basis with the damn protestors and the
security guard who hadn't changed since my first
visit more than twelve years prior. The doctor was
also the same, even though I didn't know what he
looked like since I was either put to sleep or doped
up.

I went through the usual intake and went
back for an ultrasound. After she did the scan, she
went and got another nurse. They went outside and
was whispering something. I had been there long
enough to know something was wrong. They came in
and told me that I was eighteen weeks pregnant, and
I could not get the abortion done there. They said
they had to refer me to another place. There was no
way I was eighteen weeks. How did I go that long? I
gained weight, but I wasn't showing at all. I begged
her to recheck. She even had the office manager

come in and show me. I could see the baby moving and everything. She said in a few weeks they could tell me the sex. I was so fucked. I was pregnant by Gene or Jerome, and I didn't know which one for sure. I could not be pregnant by Rudy, because he had a vasectomy. I didn't know what I was going to do.

I called the cab back and rushed her to get me back to my car. I was so paranoid at this time. I didn't know who else to call, so I decided to call Dr. Roth. He was always on standby, and he told me to come right in to see him. I was hysterical and hyperventilating, and he was so calm. How did he manage to stay so clam when I was so erratic? He told me to lay back on the couch he had in his office. The same couch that Gina had told me her whole life story on some months back. I just trusted the man for some reason and leaned back. He told me to close my eyes and go back to my childhood. I was envisioning the beautiful room I had with all those stuffed animals, and then I thought of Gina blaming me for ripping all their heads off and Daddy believing her. I started to get angry. He told me to share what I was thinking but to keep my eyes closed. So, I trusted him and did that. I told him the whole story about the stuffed animals. Then, I went on to tell him about when Gina shot Daddy and blamed me, but I stopped short of saying that.

"Go on, Brea. Trust the process," he said calmly.

I just told him, "She shot Daddy. I didn't."

I started to cry. Then, he asked me to name a person that I loved to be around when I was a child.

The first person I thought of was Tim, and I started crying some more.

"Go on," he said in a tone that just made me feel so comfortable.

I started to tell him about that dreadful time in the basement and how Tim raped me. I began to cry louder. I still had my eyes closed, and he sat by me on the couch.

"I'm here with you. You are safe, and you are loved."

I began to go through my entire life story - all the abortions, all the heartbreaks, sleeping with multiple men, P and his uncle, Pastor Vick, setting up Draya and Mike, the events that occurred in Atlanta, the suicide attempt, the HIV scare, and my current pregnancy that was not by my boyfriend but possibly by my estranged husband or the married father of my son who wasn't really my baby's dad. I didn't have to tell him about the bipolar since he was the one who diagnosed me. I let it all out. For the first time in my life, I was open and honest about my fucked up life. I was like Gina. She had made me fucked up just like her, and there was no recovering from it.

After I finished giving him my nightmare of a life story, he told me to sit up but keep my eyes closed, which I did. He began to pray over me, but not in a hallelujah kind of way. He was Jewish, and he wore that thing on his head, so I don't know what kind of prayer he was saying, but it wasn't in English. I felt a peace come over me as he prayed. He told me to open my eyes, and he hugged me.

"Brea, you have the power to change your life. No matter what you have been through, today is a new day, and you can change."

He went on to explain that I didn't need to be truthful with everyone else, I just needed to be true to myself. Who was this man? He was amazing. He had a way of making me feel at peace. He taught me some breathing techniques to help me with my anxiety. I knew I still had to figure out what I was going to do about the baby situation, but I felt like I had removed negative pieces of me. Just telling my story to someone and having them listen felt so good. He was not there to judge me, and he wasn't going to anyway. He was not going to take advantage of me. He was helping me, and he was the real deal.

He did tell me that he didn't recommend that I take the medication for my bipolar since I was pregnant. I never was consistent at taking it anyway. He made me an appointment for the following week and told me to try to get Gina to come with me. I left with some hope. I was just going to tell Rudy that when we broke up, I slept with my ex and got pregnant. He was sure to leave me, and I really wanted him to do it. I just wanted him out my life, and I shouldn't have ever invited him back in the first place. I was determined to get him out my life for good since I knew I wasn't pregnant by him.

I went about my normal day-to-day routine for the next few days. I was definitely getting bigger, and I couldn't hide it for much longer. I was scared to visit Gina, because I knew she would know. I did miss Rome, and I had started to feel the baby move a lot. I had not made a doctor's appointment just yet, because I was not ready to be a mom. I had been taking off work here and there, and I didn't care if they fired me or not, but for some reason they didn't. I was trying to avoid everyone. Rudy was staying away more and more, and I was happy. I picked Rome up from school one day and brought him back to the house, so we could have taco night. I even got us some cookies to make. Rudy had been on night shift, so I was not expecting to see him. Rome and I laughed, talked, and played. He even told me about a girl he liked. I thought it was so cute, and I just listened to him like a normal mom - not like coo-coo Gina. He asked me was Rudy coming home, and I told him no and his little face lit up.

"Mom, can I stay? I want to stay with you all the time."

I was okay with it. We called Gina, and she said it was fine as long as I had him back in the morning for school and if Rudy was working. I assured her that he was. He decided to eat cookies in my bed and watch a movie. He loved watching movies with me. Most of the time, I just fell asleep though. Rudy would usually get home at about 8 a.m., and we would be long gone by then. I actually had to be at work at 8 a.m. the next day. He fell asleep watching the movie, and I knew he was too heavy for me to carry him in his room. I just left him there, and I did something I didn't usually do. I kissed him on the cheek and just smiled. I was happy to have him there with me. When I finally got rid of Rudy, I was going to spend a lot of time with him.

The precious moment with my son didn't last long. It seemed like soon as I went to sleep, Rudy came waking me up.

"Brea, get this little muthafucker out my bed."
It wasn't his bed, I had actually bought it myself. He was drunk, and he must have been drinking on the job. He did that a lot. He was supposed to protect and serve, but all he did was break the law. I hated him. I asked him to help me carry Rome into his bed.

"Fuck no. Just wake his ass up, I'm tired."
I managed to carry him without waking him up. I laid in the bed with Rome and just prayed for God to make me a better person. I was a good person deep down inside. I just wanted out, and I just wanted to change. I made my way back to the room to find that he was taking up the whole bed with his size fifteen feet hanging off the bed. That full-size bed was not meant for a man his size. I went into the kitchen to get some snacks, and my mind started wondering. I knew I had to get rid of Rudy, because he would never let me be happy. I grabbed a steak knife out of the butcher block that was on the counter. I shut Rome's door, and I slowly crept into the bedroom. I was going to murder him. That was the only way. I saw a lifetime movie about a lady that had got off for killing her abusive husband. That's it I would kill him and plead insane or something. I did have a history of mental illness.

I walked up slowly and stood over him. I knew he wouldn't wake up, because he was a very hard sleeper. I pulled the knife back and stopped short of stabbing him in the back. I then thought maybe I should cut his throat, but I knew that little steak knife wasn't going to do it. I jogged slowly in the kitchen and got a big butcher knife. I washed it off for some reason and looked at it while touching the blade. I thought to myself that this would do the job for sure. I slowly went back into the room and stood over him again. I had the knife in both hands, and I raised my arms above my head prepared to stab him. As I went forward to stab him, the fucking alarm went off.

BUZZ BUZZZ BUZZ...

Damn it! I quickly pushed the knife under the bed and rushed to turn the alarm off. He started to move, and I was afraid he was going to wake up. I hit the snooze button and sat on the side of the bed. He didn't wake up. I slowly turned the alarm off and knew I had to get Rome up. Shit, I should have killed that nigga while I had the chance. I got the knife and put it back in the kitchen. I woke Rome up and begged him to be quiet. I told him that Rudy got off early, and he was asleep. He was instantly fearful. I told him that one day soon we would be on our own without him.

"Do you trust me, Rome?"

He shook his head yes. I got dressed and just slide anything on that I could find. I didn't care much about how I looked. I dropped him off and made it to work with a few minutes to spare. I was so hungry, so I went and got some cheese fries and a coke from the break room.

"Damn, Brea, you getting thick, girl."

One of my male coworkers shared that with me as I was leaving out. I just smiled and went to my desk. I needed to make a doctor's appointment fast, because between me taking Lithium and drinking coke, something could be terribly wrong with the baby. I made an appointment for the following day.

Rudy did not come home that night, and it felt

so nice to not have him around. I was worried about my appointment the next day, but I knew I needed to go. I was at least five months pregnant, and I needed to be checked out. I arrived nice and early and was the first one to be seen. They took my weight, and I was up to 135 pounds. Damn I had gained some more weight. They also drew blood from me and took a urine sample. The nurse proceeded to go over a laundry list of questions: how many pregnancies, how many live births, how many abortions, how many miscarriages. Damn, they were nosey. I answered untruthfully of course. I didn't need all these white folk knowing all my business. I just said that I was pregnant one time. She explained that they were testing for all STDs including HIV.

"I don't have HIV," I said in a snappy manner.

She looked at me and said, "Honey, that's great. So, you have nothing to worry about."

She told me I should have all my results in two to three days, and if I didn't hear anything, then that was good news. I wasn't really worried about that though. She then led me into a room that had an ultrasound machine that was very similar to the one at the abortion clinic. She told me to undress from the waist down. She began the ultrasound. I heard the heartbeat, and she went over every single body part with me. I don't recall getting treated this nicely when I was pregnant with Rome. She then asked me if I wanted to know the sex. At first, I was like hell no. Then, with her all happy the way she was, I decided to go ahead and find out. She was pointing at something on the screen, but I didn't see anything.

She said, "It's a girl." A girl. What was I going to do with a little girl? My own mother hated me, so I would probably hate her as well considering Gina and I were the same damn person. She then told me that I was twenty weeks and four days pregnant, and my due date was in May. I just looked confused. She told me I could get dressed and the doctor would be in to go over a few things. A girl, wow. I just shook my head and for about two minutes, I felt a sense of happiness.

The doctor just came in to go over any questions or concerns that I may have had. I did tell him about the Lithium. He expressed concern and advised me not to take it unless I felt a strong need to do so. He told me the importance of eating right and explained that the proper diet could help me with my bipolar disorder. How eating right could help was beyond me, but I listened. I asked him if vasectomies were 100%. He laughed and pointed to a picture of a baby.

"That's my vasectomy baby."

He went on to explain that he had a vasectomy many years ago and last year his wife delivered a bouncing baby boy. He explained that nothing is 100% except no sex at all. He also said the more time passed after the procedure, the lower the effective rate. He gave me so much stuff about having a baby, and he even gave me a brochure on vasectomy. He congratulated me and told me he would see me in a month. I made my way to the car, and I was wondering if there was a slight chance that Rudy could be the father. Either way, I needed to tell him and get him out of my life. I made it up in my mind that I was going to tell him for sure. I was just going to be honest like Dr. Roth said. I didn't know what I was going to say, but I had to get it out.

I went home that evening and looked over all the baby stuff I had gotten from the doctor. I heard Rudy coming, so I quickly shoved the papers into the nightstand drawer with the other millions of papers that I had stashed in there. He had never moved in officially, but he surely was over my house every day. He came into the room and immediately tried to have sex with me. I was not in the mood at all, but I just laid there and let him bust a quick nut. I told him we really needed to talk.

"Brea, I got stuff to do. I'm not ready for no marriage, woman, so don't bring that up."

This nigga was really full of himself. I was not interested in marrying him at all. I'd rather die alone than be his wife. Besides, I still had a husband. I just let him know that we needed to talk and soon. He said okay and went straight to sleep. I sat on the patio and wondered about life without Rudy and with my two kids, Rome and my unborn baby girl. What would I name her? I never thought about what to name Rome, because I was young, so I just named him after his dad. Her name had to be special. I started down the alphabet: Angela, Brianna, Carla, Diane, Eunice, Francesca, Gabrielle, Harriet, Isabelle, Justine, Kennedy, Lois, Mary, Nyla... That was it - Nyla. It just had a ring to it. Nyla. That's exactly what her name would be. I looked up at the stars and just felt like things were going to get better. I didn't know how or when, but I knew one day they would be better. They had to be.

The next morning, Rudy woke up with an attitude and picked a fight with me. He kept pushing me while I was trying to get ready for work. I only had to work four hours that day, so I just decided to call out. He kick me while I was sitting on the edge of the bed.

"Please stop. I'm not feeling well."

He started mocking me. He was extremely immature, and I didn't understand where all this was coming from out of the blue. He was so aggressive, and I hated that. Then, he tried to have a quickie with me, and I was not having it. I refused and he finally let up.

"That's cool. I'll just go fuck somebody else."

I fired back without thinking, and said, "That's fine with me."

He rushed over and choked me off the ground.

"One of these days, I'm going to kill your stupid ass, you dumb bitch."

He dropped me like I was a rag doll and walked out the door, but not before getting his gun off the mantle where he would often leave it. I laid there holding my stomach, praying that my baby was fine and wishing that I would have killed him when I had the chance.

It was the weekend and Gina and Daddy were going to come over after they did their weekly shopping and trip to the flea market. Rome wanted to see me, and I knew Rudy was at work, so it was cool. I made sure the house was completely spotless before Madame Gina arrived. I was feeling down in the dumps and extremely depressed. I made myself a spinach and shrimp salad and decided to take a nap. I was awakened by a loud bang on the door. Everyone had a key, and Gina never knocked.

I yelled, "Come on up," thinking it was Gina and Daddy.

"It's me. I don't have my key."

It was Rudy. I knew he was probably coming home to get a snack and a beer like he often did on the clock. He walked in and took my leftover salad and started eating it.

"Brea, have you seen my I.D.? They're tripping about us not having them."

"I think I saw it in the room on the nightstand," I replied.

He sat on the couch and turned the channel to sports. I turned my back to him and tried to go back to sleep, praying he left before Gina came. After about forty-five minutes of him talking loud on the phone, eating, and watching sports he finally got up and went into the room. I was acting like I was sleep, but he didn't care.

"Brea, where is my fucking I.D.? Damn, come help me."

I kicked my feet and sat up. Then, I rubbed my eyes and waddled over to the room. I got to the doorway, and all I saw was Rudy holding the ultrasound pictures and the pink paper that had my due date on it. Oh shit, I was caught.

"Bitch, you pregnant? You been fucking around on me bitch! I'm gonna kill you!"

I ran to Rome's room and locked the door. He was pushing on it, and then, he began kicking it.

"Bitch, you pregnant! I'm gonna kill you!"

I yelled back, "Rudy, there is still a chance to produce sperm after a vasectomy! Look at all the papers."

Now, in the back of my mind I was not 100% sure he was the father. As a matter of fact, I was almost 100% sure that he wasn't, but in that moment, I had to say what I could to save my life. It got quiet, but I knew he was still there. I looked out the window, and his patrol car was still double parked. I kept calling his name and telling him that we could make it work if he would just calm down and listen to what I had to say. He started banging on the door and screaming.

"If I get in this room, bitch, I'm gonna kill you."

I wanted to go out the window, but Rome's room did not have a large window. Pre-pregnancy Brea would have been able to fit through that window with no problems, but pregnant Brea couldn't fit. I was stuck with no way out, and he was kicking the door even harder. I could hear it coming off the hinges. He finally busted open the door. BOOM! He had a thick black belt in his hand, and he was slapping it on the wall.

"Rudy, please listen to me. I'm pregnant with your child, and I know it sounds crazy. Just look at the papers the doctor gave me."

He refused to even listen, and I saw the devil in his eyes. I got into a fetal position in the corner to protect the baby. He began to repeatedly hit me over and over again with the thick belt. Then, he started kicking me and spitting on me.

"Bitch, you gone die today."

I didn't even want to fight back, because I really wanted to protect the baby. He punched me in my face, and then kicked me into a semi-unconscious state causing me to blackout. As I regained consciousness, he was straddled over me still smacking me in my face.

"I was a real man, girl. I was as real as it gets, and you fucked around on me."

I was trying not to lose consciousness, but I could feel my lips were swelling up.

"Rudy, please I'm pregnant with our little girl. If I die, she dies. Please stop."

He just sat, looked at me, and started crying.

"See what you made me do? Now I'm going to have to kill you for real, Brea. I told you to just listen."

The tears were streaming down my face as well. Then, he took his humungous hands and wrapped them around my neck and began to choke the life out of me. I saw my past and my future pass before my eyes. I pictured a pretty little girl, and I was pushing her on the swing while Rome was playing on the sliding board. Suddenly, I heard a loud BANG! It sounded like giant firecracker on the 4th of July.

I thought I was dead until I heard, "Brea! Brea, is he dead?"

It was Gina's voice. But, why did she follow me to heaven or hell, or wherever I had gone? I sat up and gained my composure. I saw Daddy at the door. I looked and saw Gina with Rome's head in her chest as she was kneeling. I reached over to check Rudy's pulse, and he didn't have one. He was dead. I looked at the doorway and saw Rome with the gun in his hand. Rome had just killed Rudy with his police-issued weapon that he left on the mantle. Everyone was silent. I reached into Rome's laundry basket and got the dirty towel he used after he took a shower. I crawled over and took the gun from Rome. He was petrified. I wiped the gun down. Then, I stood up and pointed the gun at Rudy and shot him again.

Gina said, "Brea, oh my God! Rome just killed Rudy."

I looked at her with a sigh of relief and whispered, "No, I did."

To be continued...

ABOUT THE AUTHOR

Sammodah Hudson is a force to be reckoned with. She is the promoter of positivity, serial motivator, and author. Her purpose in life is to inspire those who are feeling hopeless, alone and uninspired, with her speaking and writings one word at a time.

She has spent many years mentoring others and helping them find what is great within. She prides herself in helping people find their true selves and live in their truth with no excuses or regrets. She was a freelance writer for many years and even helped ghost write a few novels. She finally decided to put her writings to work for herself and penned her debut novel Never Knew Love.

Sammodah is a diehard Jersey girl who happens to live Atlanta, GA. She is a wife and proud mother of 4 beautiful children. She is currently working on becoming a Certified Life Coach as well as a Best Selling Author. She has definitely put in the hard work to achieve the goals that so many are afraid to do. She loves to hear from her readers so feel free to visit the website and sign up for updates at www.sammodahspeaks.com.